Friends for Life

Friends for Life

Andrew Norriss

David Fickling Books

SCHOLASTIC INC. / NEW YORK

First published in the United Kingdom in 2015 as *Jessica's Ghost* by David Fickling Books, 31 Beaumont Street, Oxford, OX1 2NP. *www.davidficklingbooks.com*

Library of Congress Cataloging-in-Publication Data

Norriss, Andrew, author.
[Jessica's ghost]
Friends for life / Andrew Norriss.—First edition.
pages cm
"First published in the United Kingdom in 2015 as *Jessica's Ghost* by David Fickling Books."
Summary: Francis Meredith is a boy who is interested in fashion and costuming, which has made him a target at school, but when he meets Jessica his life begins to change.
ISBN 978-0-545-85186-2
1. Friendship—Juvenile fiction. 2. Costume design—Juvenile fiction. 3. Suicide—Juvenile fiction. 4. Identity (Psychology)—Juvenile fiction. 5. Ghost stories. [1. Friendship—Fiction. 2. Ghosts—Fiction. 3. Suicide—Fiction. 4. Identity—Fiction. 5. Costume design—Fiction.] I. Title.

PZ7.N7998Fr 2015
823.92—dc23
[Fic]

2015002107

10 9 8 7 6 5 4 3 2   15 16 17 18 19

Printed in the U.S.A.   23
First edition, September 2015

For all the Jessicas
and the people who loved them.

1

Francis needed to be alone.

He needed to be alone so that he could think, which was why, despite the weather, he carried his bag and his lunch to a bench on the far side of the playing field.

Solitude is not always easy to find in a busy school, but it was February, the temperature was barely above freezing, and the cold, Francis knew, would keep most people indoors. And if anyone did come out, they would probably avoid that particular bench. It was directly opposite the main school building, and students at John Felton usually preferred to spend their lunch break somewhere that was not in full view of the teachers' lounge and the school office.

Francis did not mind being watched—not from that distance, anyway. All he wanted was the chance to think without any distractions. And he was sitting on the bench, his hat pulled firmly down over his ears, holding a cup of hot tea in chilled fingers . . . when a distraction came walking across the grass toward him.

It was a girl about his own age—though not anyone he recognized as being at the school—and possibly the most distracting thing about her was what she was wearing.

Or rather, what she wasn't.

Despite the cold, she had no coat. All she had on was a little black-and-white-striped dress—someone who knew about such things would have recognized it as a Victoria Beckham zebra dress—that left her arms and shoulders exposed to the winter air. Wherever she was heading, Francis thought, there were good odds she would freeze to death before she got there.

From the corner of his eye he watched as, to his surprise, the girl continued to walk directly toward him until she stopped, and then sat down on the other end of the bench. The wooden slats were still coated with frost, but this did not seem to trouble her. She sat there, and stared calmly out across the field at the building on the far side, without uttering a word.

Francis had not wanted company, but he was curious. Why had she come across the field to sit beside him? Why had she not spoken? And why was she apparently immune to the cold?

"You might want some of this," he said, holding out his mug. "It's only tea, but it's warm."

The girl turned to face him, then turned her head in the opposite direction, as if to see who he was talking to. When she realized there was nobody else, and that he must have been talking to her, a look of shocked surprise crossed her face.

"Are you . . . are you talking to me?" she asked.

"Sorry." Francis withdrew the offered mug. "Won't happen again."

"You can hear me as well?"

"Yes," said Francis. "Sorry about that, too."

The girl frowned. "But nobody can see me! Or hear me!"

"Can't they?"

"Unless . . ." The girl peered at him intently. "You're not dead as well, are you?"

"I don't think so."

Francis did his best to keep smiling while he quietly emptied the remains of his tea onto the grass and screwed the cup back onto the thermos. It felt like it might be time to pack up and leave.

"I don't understand . . ." The girl was still staring at him.

"You're . . . um . . . you're dead yourself, are you?" Francis tried to keep a casual tone in his voice as he packed his thermos into his bag.

"What? Oh . . . yes." As if to illustrate her point, the girl lifted an arm and ran it through the planks that made up the back of the bench as if they had no more substance than smoke. "But I don't understand why you can see me. I mean . . . nobody can!"

For several seconds, Francis did not move. Frozen, with the thermos in one hand and his bag in the other, his brain replayed, on a loop, the action he had just witnessed.

"In all the time I've been dead," said the girl, "no one—I mean *no one*—has been able to see me or hear me. Not ever."

"Would you mind," said Francis slowly, "doing that again? The thing with your arm? Through the bench?"

"What, this?" The girl repeated the action of brushing her arm through the wooden slats behind her.

"Yes. Thank you."

The girl looked briefly puzzled, but then her face

cleared. "Oh! You wanted to check you hadn't just imagined it!" she said.

"Yes," said Francis.

"Well, you didn't," said the girl. "I'm definitely dead, but nobody's been able to see me before. I mean, I've stood in front of people and screamed, but none of them ever . . ." She looked across at Francis. "But you can?"

Francis managed to nod.

"Well, that is just *weird*!" said the girl. "I mean, you walk around for a year, totally invisible, and then you sit down on a bench and the . . ." She looked across at Francis. "You gave me quite a fright!" She paused again before adding, "I suppose it must have been a bit of a shock for you, too."

"It was a bit," said Francis. "Still is, really."

"I don't understand it." The girl shook her head. "No one's ever been able to see me. I mean . . . I'm dead!"

"How?" asked Francis.

"What?"

"I just wondered how you'd died."

"Oh, I see." The girl gave a little shrug. "I can't remember that bit. I suppose I must have been killed in an accident or something. All I know is I found myself at the hospital one evening, and I was . . ."

"Dead?" suggested Francis.

"Yes."

"And nobody could see you or hear you . . ."

"No."

"Right . . . That must have been . . . Right . . ."

There was a long silence, which was eventually broken by the sound of the school bell signaling the end of lunch break.

"That bell means you have to go in to class, doesn't it?" said the girl.

Francis agreed that it did. He picked up his lunch box and put it in his bag, but made no move to leave.

"The thing is . . ." said the girl, "I wonder . . . would you mind coming back? After?"

"You mean at the end of school?"

"Yes. I don't mind waiting. Like I said, nobody's been able to see me or hear me before. And it's . . . good to have someone to talk to."

"Okay," said Francis.

"You don't mind?"

"No." Francis stood up and pulled the bag on to his shoulder. "No, that . . . that'd be fine."

He took a few steps in the direction of the school.

"I'm Jessica," said the girl. "Jessica Fry."

"Francis," said Francis. "Francis Meredith."

On his way back to the main building, it briefly crossed his mind to skip class, go to the office, and tell someone what had just happened. He wondered what they would do. Would they call the hospital? His mother? A psychiatrist?

Not that it mattered, he thought, because he had no intention of telling anyone that he had just met a ghost on his lunch break.

He had quite enough problems without claiming he could see dead people.

2

When he came out of school at three fifteen and saw Jessica waiting for him on the bench, Francis's first feeling was one of relief. A part of him had half expected to discover that the meeting at lunchtime had been some sort of delusion, and the sight of Jessica, waiting as she had promised, was oddly reassuring.

She had, he saw, changed her clothes. The zebra dress had gone and she was now wearing jeans and a puffer coat, with a pair of Uggs on her feet and a knitted hat on her head. She stood up as he approached.

"Hi," she said.

"Hi." Francis stopped in front of her.

There was a slightly awkward pause.

"If we try and talk out here," said Jessica, "you'll freeze. Is there somewhere we could go?"

"You could come home if you like," suggested Francis. "That is . . . if you can. Are ghosts allowed to move around?"

"I don't know about other ghosts," said Jessica, "but this one can go where she wants. Is it far?"

"About five minutes. I live on Alma Road." Francis led the way toward the school entrance. "You changed."

"You mean the clothes?"

"Yes. How does that work exactly? You have like a . . . a ghost wardrobe somewhere?"

"I can wear whatever I like," said Jessica. "When I first found I was dead, I was in this hospital gown, and it was weeks before I realized I didn't have to be." She glanced across at Francis. "I just have to think about it."

"That's all? You just think?"

"It takes a bit of concentration," said Jessica, "but . . . yes."

She paused midstride for a moment, there was a faint blurring around her body, and the jeans and puffer coat disappeared, to be replaced by the zebra dress she had been wearing earlier.

"That . . . is a neat trick," said Francis.

"I saw a picture of it in a magazine someone was reading," said Jessica, "and I thought . . . why not? You can't feel the cold when you're a ghost, you see."

"Useful," said Francis.

"And it's kind of fun." Jessica switched back to the jeans and coat. "You see something you like, no need to wonder how much it would cost. Just think yourself into it."

"So it's not all bad?" said Francis. "The being dead thing, I mean."

"Well, it's not what I expected." Jessica frowned. "Not that I expected anything, really. I thought once you died that was the end, and everything stopped. Nobody ever warned me I could wind up as a ghost." She paused. "But I suppose it's all right, once you get used to it. It's . . . kind of peaceful, you know?"

"Peaceful is good," Francis agreed.

"A bit lonely sometimes, but I never get tired, or hungry. There's nobody telling me where to go or how to behave. I can do whatever I want."

"And what do you do?"

"Oh, you know . . . go here and there." Jessica waved an arm vaguely in the direction of the town. "There's things going on all over the place, and I can watch any of it."

"But you can't talk to anyone."

"No."

"Not even other ghosts?"

"I've never met any other ghosts," said Jessica. "I don't even know if there are any. Which is odd, if you think about it." She looked carefully at Francis. "It doesn't bother you, does it?"

"What?"

"Me being a ghost."

Francis considered this. He had been bothered, when he first saw Jessica, that she might be crazy—or that he might be going crazy himself—but when she had put her arm through the back of the bench to show that she was a ghost . . . that part hadn't bothered him at all. Surprised him, certainly, but not bothered.

"I think if I'd seen a ghost," said Jessica, "you know, when I was alive, I'd have run a mile. But I could see it didn't really worry you, did it?"

"No," said Francis. "No, it didn't."

It had probably helped, he thought, that it had all happened in daylight—out in the sunshine with the sounds of a busy school in the background—but it wasn't just that. There was something about the girl walking beside him that made it impossible to be frightened of her. Everything about her—apart from the fact that she was dead—was too *normal* to be scary.

It also helped that, for some reason, he liked her.

"I suppose," said Jessica, "you're one of those strong, silent types who aren't really frightened of anything."

"Oh, definitely." Francis pushed open a gate and led the way up the path to the door of a tall, redbrick, Victorian terraced house.

"Mr. Fearless. That's me."

● ● ●

Jessica followed Francis into a narrow hallway, dominated by an enormous oil painting in an elaborate gilt frame. It was a full-length portrait of a severe-looking man in naval uniform, with gold epaulets on his shoulders and one hand resting on the sword at his waist.

"Wow," she said. "Who's he?"

"The Admiral." Francis pulled off his coat and hung it on a stand. "My great-great-grandfather."

He picked up his bag and headed for the stairs.

"I just have to get changed. Won't be a minute."

He went up the stairs two at a time and, in his bedroom, quickly changed from school clothes into jeans and a T-shirt. He came out to find Jessica waiting for him on the landing. She had gotten rid of the puffer coat and the woolen hat, and was wearing a loosely fitting knitted top with the jeans.

She was looking at another portrait, almost as large as the one in the hall downstairs, but this time of a young woman in a dress from the 1920s. She was standing with one arm resting on a rather grand fireplace, looking out of the picture and laughing.

"Who's this one?" she asked.

"Great-grandmother," said Francis. "The Admiral's favorite daughter."

Jessica nodded as she continued to study the painting.

"You can tell a lot about people from the clothes they're wearing, can't you?" she said. "The Admiral downstairs, for instance. His uniform's all buttoned up, and it holds him in, like all the rules he has to obey." She gestured to the picture in front of her. "But what she's wearing is loose and free. You can see she's not held in by anything, and she likes it."

She turned to Francis, as if expecting him to say something. But he didn't.

"Sorry. I forgot. Boys aren't really interested in clothes, are they?" She moved toward the stairs. "Are we going back down?"

"I just have to put this in my room." Francis was holding his schoolbag and heading toward another, narrower flight of stairs that led up rather than down.

"I thought that was your room." Jessica pointed to the bedroom.

"That's where I sleep," said Francis. "I have another room upstairs for . . . other stuff."

"Can I see?"

Francis very nearly said no. In fact, the words were already forming in his head to explain why she couldn't—that there was nothing up there, that they'd be more comfortable down in the kitchen, that he was hungry and needed something to eat—but for some reason those were not the words that came out. He never really knew why. Except that it seemed to be one of those days when the ordinary rules did not apply.

"Sure," he said. "Why not?"

3

Francis led the way through a door at the top of the stairs into a room that ran the entire length of the house.

The first thing Jessica noticed were the drawings taped to the wall in front of her. They were fashion designs, done mostly in pen and ink, for a series of coats, dresses, and gowns. Beneath them was a workbench with a sewing machine, and stacked beneath that were rolls of material in a kaleidoscope of patterns and colors. To the left, under a skylight, was a table covered in a length of off-white cotton with parts of a paper pattern laid out on top. To the right, a dressmaker's dummy stood at one end of a battered leather sofa.

They were not the sorts of things you might expect to find in a boy's room but, most surprising of all, and only visible when she stepped into the room and looked behind her, was a set of shelves on which were displayed several rows of dolls. There were at least fifty of them, each dressed in a different outfit.

"What is this place?" she asked.

"I told you." Francis's voice was studiedly neutral, but he was watching Jessica carefully as he spoke. "It's mine. It's where I do stuff."

Jessica walked over to the shelves with the dolls.

"So all these are yours?"

"Yes." Francis came over to join her. "I was trying to make a sort of illustrated history of fashion in the last fifty years." He picked up one of the dolls. It was dressed in a studded leather jacket and had its hair cropped and dyed in the pattern of the American flag. "Each doll represents a particular style, you see? Fly girl, punk, grunge . . ."

Jessica pointed to a doll dressed in a suit of what looked like molded pink plastic. "What's that one?"

"It's a Miyake," said Francis. "Japanese designer."

Jessica turned away from the dolls for a moment and gestured to the drawings pinned on the wall opposite. "And those are all yours as well?"

Francis nodded. "I'm interested in fashion. Always have been."

Jessica stared around her, and then her face broke into a smile. "I would have killed to have a place like this when I was alive!" she said.

Francis did not reply directly, but something in his shoulders and his face seemed to relax for the first time since they had entered the room.

"Let's talk about fashion later," he said. "First, I need to know more about being a ghost."

He put the doll with the cropped hair back on the shelf and walked over to the sofa.

"So tell me," he said as he sat down. "How did it start?"

• • •

It had started, as far as Jessica could remember, with finding herself standing at the window of a small room on the third floor of the hospital, looking out through the darkness at a parking garage on the other side of the road.

Although she could not remember how it had happened, she had known at once that she was dead. She knew it in the same way that she knew that the body under the sheet on the bed beside her had once been hers. She did not need to see the face, or read the messages on the little cards attached to the bunches of flowers. She just knew.

Being dead, as she had told Francis earlier, did not worry her particularly. She was not in any pain or discomfort and the predominant feeling was a general sensation of calm and quiet. When the nurses came to take away the body, she had felt no inclination to follow them. It was, after all, only a body.

What did puzzle her, though, was what she was supposed to *do*, now that she was dead. After standing by the window for what felt like several hours, she had, for lack of anything better to do, drifted out into the corridor and then explored other parts of the hospital. She had quickly discovered that she could move through walls and doors, float up through ceilings and sink down through floors as easily as if they did not exist, and such freedom of movement might have been rather enjoyable if . . .

. . . if she had not had the nagging feeling that she had *missed* something.

"Missed what?" asked Francis.

"I don't know." Jessica's forehead wrinkled as she searched for the best words to describe how she had felt. "It was like I knew I was supposed to do *something*, only I didn't know what. And there wasn't anyone who could tell me."

"So what did you do?"

"Well, I thought maybe whoever was supposed to tell me hadn't been able to because I'd been wandering around the hospital, so I went back to the room on the third floor and waited."

"Waited?"

"Yes."

"For how long?"

"In a way, I suppose I'm still waiting." Jessica sighed. "Not all the time, obviously. During the day I go out and do stuff. But I always go back to the hospital in the evening. It's not like I *have* to, but . . . well, it *is* a bit like that, I suppose."

"And you think one day someone will turn up and tell you what to do?" asked Francis.

"Who knows?" Jessica gave a little shrug. "I just have this feeling that, if anything's going to happen, it'll be there. In that room."

"And you've been going back there every night . . . for a year?"

"Yes."

Francis gave a sympathetic whistle. "A year's a long time."

"I know."

For a while, neither of them spoke, and then Jessica pointed around her to the dolls and the drawings on the walls.

"Anyway, your turn. When did all this start?"

Francis was about to answer when he was interrupted by the sound of the front door opening and someone calling from downstairs.

"That's Mum," he said. "Hang on. I'll be right back."

Francis got down to the landing on the second floor in time to see his mother, a tall, untidy-looking woman, taking off her coat in the hallway and hanging it up on the stand.

"How did it go?" asked Francis, leaning over the banister.

"Could have been worse. Sold two plates!" His mother looked up at him and smiled. "How was your day?"

"It was okay."

"No . . . trouble or anything?"

"No. No trouble."

"Good." Francis's mother was heading toward the

kitchen. "I think there's a pizza left in the freezer. I'll call you when it's ready, okay?"

Francis went back upstairs to the attic, where he found Jessica dressed as she had been when they arrived, in the puffer coat, Ugg boots, and knitted hat.

"I'd better be going," she said.

"You don't have to," Francis assured her. "I'll need to go and eat at some point, but—"

"It's getting late," Jessica interrupted him. "I ought to get back to the hospital." She hesitated before adding. "But I could see you tomorrow. If you like."

"Definitely," said Francis. "Lunchtime? Same place?"

"Okay."

Francis moved to the stairway—he had some vague idea of walking Jessica to the front door—but she made no attempt to follow. Instead, she stared down at the carpet, seemingly lost in thought.

"Do you have any idea," she said eventually, "why you can see me, when no one else can?"

"No," said Francis. "Do you?"

"Not really." Jessica looked up. "But I did wonder if maybe you were the one who could tell me what I was meant to do next."

"I'm sorry," said Francis. "I wish I could, but I don't know anything about . . . ghosts. I don't know anything about anything, really. Except clothes."

"No . . . well, never mind." Jessica smiled. "I'll see you tomorrow, then."

And she disappeared.

4

When Francis walked across the playing field at lunch break the next day, Jessica was sitting on the bench waiting for him, dressed in a salmon-pink party dress.

"It's what a woman was wearing when she came into the hospital last night," she said, standing up to give him a twirl that revealed half a dozen petticoats. "Do you like it?"

"I do," said Francis admiringly. "Most impressive."

"It's a Sarah Burton."

"Even more impressive," said Francis. Sarah Burton was one of his favorite designers, though this was not an outfit he recognized. "How do you know?"

"I checked the label when they were undressing her." Jessica sat down, patting the dress over her legs. "I really ought to be wearing jewelry with it, like she was, but I can't do jewelry. I don't know why. I can do shoes and hair, no problem, but when I try and imagine jewelry . . . nothing happens."

Francis sat down beside her.

"So that's what ghosts do in the evenings, is it? Hang around in the emergency room and check out what the patients are wearing?"

"It's not the *only* thing," said Jessica. "I like watching the operations and stuff as well. But I like seeing what people wear. I've always liked clothes. Even when I was little, I preferred watching Tim Gunn on TV to Peppa Pig. That's what my gran said, anyway. And my favorite toy was always the dress-up box."

Francis said that he had never had a dress-up box, but that he could still remember the excitement of finding his mother's copies of *Vogue*, and how he had carried them away to his room and looked at nothing else for days. That was when he was four. When he was eight, he had asked for a sewing machine for his birthday so that he could begin making his own versions of the designs he copied from magazines or had seen in shopwindows.

Sitting on the bench in the wintry sunshine, while Francis ate his sandwiches and drank his thermos of tea, they discovered that an interest in clothes was not the only thing they had in common. They were, for a start, almost exactly the same age—not counting Jessica's year as a ghost—with birthdays only a week apart. They were both "only" children. They had both been brought up by single mothers, and both had had to move house unexpectedly, when they were twelve, and had not enjoyed it at all.

"I wonder," said Jessica, "if that's why you can see me. Because we're so alike."

"Not that alike," said Francis. "One of us is dead, remember?"

"You know what I mean!" Jessica poked him with a ghostly elbow that disappeared several inches into his coat. "Having all those things in common . . . it can't just be a coincidence, can it?"

They were still debating the possibility when the bell rang for the start of class, and it seemed only natural that, when Francis went to his class, Jessica should go with him.

She sat in a chair beside him, and although conversation was limited—at least for Francis, who had to be careful how and when he spoke to someone no one else could see—they both rather enjoyed it.

Jessica was useful, too. In the pop quiz in Mrs. Archer's history class, Jessica was able to check around the class to see what everyone else was writing. And in Mr. Williams's math class that followed, she was able to give Francis a wonderfully clear explanation of integer inequalities. The fact that she did it while wearing an exact copy of Mr. Williams's shiny blue suit with all the pens in his top pocket made even that lesson . . . kind of fun.

• • •

Later, back at the attic room on Alma Road, Jessica asked what he was working on at the moment, and Francis showed her the table covered in a length of off-white cotton cloth with part of a paper pattern pinned to the top.

"It's some cotton pinpoint I was given," he explained, "and I thought I'd try and make a top." He reached for a sketchbook and flipped it open. "That's the design."

"Neat," said Jessica. "Who's it for?"

"Betty." Francis pointed to the dressmaker's dummy standing by the sofa. "It's just an exercise, really. Practice, you know."

Privately, Jessica thought it was a shame that a dummy would be the only person ever to wear the clothes Francis made, but she said nothing. Instead she talked—mostly about fashion and the styles she liked and the ones she didn't—while Francis draped the pieces of a paper pattern over the dressmaker's dummy to check the size, and then pinned the result to the material spread out on the table before cutting them out.

He worked with an easy confidence that Jessica could not help but admire, and it was an hour or so later, seeing him hunched over the sewing machine running down a seam, that she noticed him pause for a moment to stretch his shoulders in a different direction. He's getting a cramp, she thought, like Gran used to do. Forgetting for a moment that she was a ghost, she reached out to massage the muscles at the bottom of his neck.

Immediately, Francis stopped and turned around. "Was that you?" he asked.

"Um . . . yes . . ." Even without a body, Jessica could feel herself blushing. "I was going to rub your shoulders. It's what I used to do for my gran."

"But I could feel you!" Francis was puzzled. "How could I feel you touching me if you're a ghost?"

"I don't know." Jessica reached forward, put her hands on his shoulders, and pushed her thumbs along the muscles of his neck. They disappeared beneath his skin. "You can feel that?"

"Oh, yes . . ." Francis leaned back so that the thumbs went even deeper, and closed his eyes. It was a strange but definitely pleasant sensation, relaxing and yet somehow invigorating at the same time. As if he were sitting out in the sun on a summer's day, and the warmth was soaking through to his bones.

"Wow . . ." he said. "You are just full of surprises, aren't you?"

• • •

The next day, they met in the morning rather than at lunchtime. Francis came out of the house at quarter to nine and found Jessica waiting for him on the sidewalk, and they walked in to school together, went to class together, hung out together at recess, and returned, when school had finished, to the room at the top of the house on Alma Road.

After almost twelve hours in each other's company, neither of them showed any signs of being bored. In that curious way these things happen sometimes, they seemed to fit together.

Which was why they did the same thing the day after . . .

And the day after . . .

And the day after that.

● ● ●

If someone had asked Francis if he didn't think spending most of his waking hours with a ghost was a bit . . . odd, he would probably have agreed that it was. But he didn't care. As the days passed, he hardly thought of Jessica as a ghost. She was simply . . . his friend. She was also the only person his own age he had ever met who could talk about synthetic fabrics as easily as most people talk about the weather, who knew the difference between a pleat and a dart, and who could recognize a Sarah Burton design when its owner was brought into the emergency room.

Compared to all that, the fact that she was dead seemed unimportant.

As for Jessica, you would probably have to have been dead for a year yourself—with no one able to see or hear you—to understand how much it meant to her to have Francis to talk to. She had not properly realized how lonely her life—or rather, her death—had been, and now she had found someone who was not only able to talk to her but was clever and funny and interesting . . .

Her only worry was that, at some point, he might want to go back to being with people who were alive—though fortunately Francis showed no signs of that at present. When she asked him once if being with her was keeping him away from his other friends, he replied, simply, that there was no one else he wanted to be with.

And it was true that he made very little effort to speak to anyone else while he was in school. For that matter, no one else seemed to make any particular effort to speak to him.

Except for Quentin, of course.

But he was not someone you could describe as a friend.

5

The first time Jessica saw Quentin Howard was when she and Francis were waiting in the corridor before going into a science lesson.

Jessica was floating six feet in the air to avoid the crowd—it made her slightly queasy to have too many people walking through her—when a thickset boy with glasses came up to Francis, holding out a battered-looking doll with one leg and no hair.

"Present for you, Francis," he said. "Found her in the road outside. She'll need some new clothes, but you're the man for that, aren't you!" And he tucked the doll into the top pocket of Francis's blazer, while everyone around him laughed.

Francis took the doll out of his pocket and was about to throw it in the trash when Mr. Nicholls, the science teacher, appeared and told him to put it away and get into the classroom. Everyone laughed again.

"What was all that about?" asked Jessica, floating down to join Francis as he made his way to a bench.

"That was Quentin," said Francis. "It's nothing. It's what he always does."

And Quentin always did. He would make a point, whenever he saw Francis, of asking if he'd bought any new dolls recently, or made any little dresses for them, or knitted them some nice underwear. Francis didn't seem to mind too much, but Jessica did.

"He's being horrid," she said, after Quentin had asked Francis at the start of a geography lesson if he ever had little tea parties with his dolls. "You should do something."

Francis only smiled. "Like what?"

"Well, for a start, you could tell him to stop."

"He's not going to stop just because I tell him to. He's enjoying himself too much for that." Francis gave a little shrug. "And anyway . . . it's partly my fault."

"*Your* fault? How?"

"I brought some sewing into school once. And Quentin found a doll in my bag."

"One of the costume dolls?"

Francis nodded. "If it had been one of the punks or something, I might have gotten away with it . . . but it was the Moschino."

"Ah." Jessica winced. Moschino was a designer who liked to put little rosettes and lace edging on the clothes he made.

"I thought of trying to tell him who Moschino was and why I liked him," said Francis, "but I had a feeling it wouldn't really help. Mum says if I take no notice, he'll give up with the teasing, eventually."

There was, Jessica thought, little sign of Quentin giving up any time soon. As Francis said, he was enjoying himself too much for that. But she still thought something should be done. Quentin's teasing—if that's what you could call it—might not worry Francis particularly, but for some reason it left her feeling distinctly uncomfortable. Francis might be one of those lucky people who never worry much about anything—the sort of person who could meet a ghost one lunchtime and simply offer them a mug of tea—but she was not made like that herself.

That, at least, was what she thought, and it was something of a shock to discover how far it was from the truth.

$\bullet \quad \bullet \quad \bullet$

They had walked into town together after school on Wednesday. Francis needed some buttons for the cotton top he was making, and he bought them in the haberdasher's section of Dummer's department store. While he was paying, Jessica floated off to look at a display of skirts and dresses on the other side of the aisle.

Although it was February, the first of the summer fashions were already making an appearance and, as Francis came out with his bag of buttons, Jessica called him over to look at a halter-neck dress priced at an ambitious £800.

Francis joined her, looked at the dress, and then reached up a hand to feel the fabric between his finger and thumb.

As he did so, a sales assistant appeared in front of him.

"Aren't you Francis Meredith?" she asked.

Francis let go of the material with a start.

"We haven't met," said the woman, "but I'm Lorna Gilchrist's mother."

Lorna was a girl in Francis's study group at school.

"I thought I recognized you from the class photo,"

the woman continued. "You're the boy who's interested in fashion, right?"

Francis did not reply.

"I'm expecting Lorna to be here soon," the woman went on. "I don't know if the two of you would like to . . ."

"I'm sorry." Francis had begun backing toward the exit. "I have to go. I'm late for . . . I'm late."

He broke into a run as he headed for the stairs and Jessica followed him out of the store, into the precinct, and watched as he slumped down on a bench, his head in his hands.

Puzzled, she sat down beside him.

"What's the matter?" she asked. "Is something wrong?"

Francis briefly lifted his head to look at her. "That was Lorna's mother."

"I know it was. I heard her telling you. But I still don't understand why you ran away. What's going on?"

"What's going on," said Francis wearily, "is that Lorna's mother will tell Lorna what she saw, won't she? And then tomorrow Lorna will tell her friends at school and everyone will know that I was seen hanging around the women's section of a department store."

"That's what's bothering you?" Jessica stared at him. "That Lorna might tell everyone tomorrow that you were seen looking at a dress?"

"Not just looking," said Francis. "Touching it as well. And yes. That is what's bothering me."

And it clearly was. His face was pale and there were little red spots in his cheeks. He looked... *frightened*.

Jessica was surprised as well as puzzled. In all the time they had been together, she had never seen her friend like this. He was Mr. Cool. Mr. Fearless. Nothing frightened Francis! Even when he met a ghost, all he did was invite her home with him. She had never seen Francis bothered by anything, and yet... here he was... *very* bothered.

"I don't get it!" she said. "Even if Lorna *did* tell someone... so what? Everyone already knows you're a bit weird when it comes to clothes, don't they!"

"Thanks," said Francis. "That really helps."

"You know what I mean! You were just looking at a dress! It's not illegal, and everyone knows you're interested in fashion. You're the guy who makes dresses for dolls for goodness' sake!"

"Yes, and now people are going to say that I'm—"

"Oh, who cares what they say?" interrupted Jessica. "Let them say what they want. It doesn't matter! Honestly. How could you think it *did*?"

She said this, or something like it, a good many times and in a dozen different ways on the walk home, with the result that, by the time they got back to Alma Road, Francis was prepared to admit that he might have overreacted. Perhaps Jessica was right. Everyone at school already knew about his interest in fashion. Maybe being seen in the women's department at Dummer's was not such a big deal. Certainly not compared with someone finding a doll in your schoolbag and realizing that you made the clothes for it . . .

He was a little less certain the next morning as he made his way in to school. If he had not had Jessica, still firmly upbeat, beside him, he might not have gone in at all, but when he got there . . .

. . . nothing happened.

If Lorna's mother had said anything to her daughter about finding Francis admiring a dress in the department store, Lorna herself did not repeat the fact to anyone else. Neither then, nor later. There was a moment, at the end of morning classes, when it looked as if she might be coming over to speak to him, but he pretended to be reading his book and she turned and left the room.

Neither Jessica nor Francis ever spoke about it afterward, but the incident made Jessica realize that Francis worried about what other people thought and said, a lot more than he let on.

6

Francis's mother had always known that her son was different from other boys. As he got older, she had seen the difference become more pronounced and was not surprised to hear that he was having problems at school. Life at a provincial middle school for a boy whose hobby was designing dresses was never going to be easy, even before he was foolish enough to let someone find a doll in his schoolbag.

Grace Meredith was a potter. In her studio—a ramshackle glass structure that extended out from the kitchen at the back of the house—she threw plates, bowls, and pots on her wheel, fired and glazed them in a kiln, and packed up the results so that they could be sold.

Working with clay was something Mrs. Meredith had always enjoyed, though she had never expected to have to earn a living from it. As a child, art had been the only subject in which she had shown any talent at school. She had followed up her interest with a brief spell at art college and, after her marriage, her new husband, David, had actually built her a studio so that she could carry on "playing with mud," as he cheerfully put it. It was only after David, a fanatical hang glider, flew into the side of a mountain and killed himself that Mrs. Meredith had been forced to think of pottery as anything more than a hobby.

With a strictly limited income, and a child and a large house to maintain, she had looked around for a way to earn some money, and selling the bowls and plates she made had seemed the obvious answer. Everyone who saw her work told her how good it was—and they were right. But unfortunately Mrs. Meredith was a better potter than she was a businesswoman, and money had remained an almost constant worry. The year before, they had had to downsize drastically to cut back on expenses. Moving to the terraced house on Alma Road had helped, but money, or rather the lack of it, was still a worrying issue.

Almost as worrying as having a son like Francis.

She had done what she could to help. She had written to the school to ask if anything could be done about the teasing. The principal had called back to say she had spoken to Francis's teacher, who had promised to keep an eye on things. The teacher had phoned a week later to say she thought the situation was improving. Francis himself assured her that this was true, but Mrs. Meredith was not entirely convinced.

Her particular worry at the moment was the amount of time her son spent on his own. As far as she could tell, in the last two weeks he had spoken to almost no one apart from her—and he hadn't done very much of that. He went to school on his own, he came home on his own and went straight up to his room in the attic, where he stayed all evening. Alone.

He came down for meals, but even then there was a *vague* look about him, as if he were listening to some voice in his head that only he could hear. Recently, she had heard him talking to himself. Creeping up to sit on the stairs outside the attic, she had put her ear to the door and heard the murmur of an entire conversation, as if he was pretending he had somebody in there with him.

It was all very worrying.

What her son needed, she knew, was to be with someone his own age. If there was someone he could walk to school with, sit with in class, talk to during the day, he might be able to get through a difficult time without too much damage.

What Francis needed was a friend, and as luck would have it, she had just found a possible candidate.

● ● ●

"You know the woman who's just moved in down the road?" Mrs. Meredith was in her studio, carefully painting the outline of a swan on the center of a plate as she spoke. "It turns out she has a son almost exactly the same age as you."

"Oh, yes?" Francis was next door in the kitchen. Jessica had gone back to the hospital, and he was making himself a hot chocolate before going to bed.

"His name's Andy." Mrs. Meredith dipped her brush in the glaze and stroked out the shape of the swan's neck. "But his mother's a bit worried about him."

"Right . . ." Francis was only half listening. Jessica had suggested before she left that they go to an exhibition of theatrical costumes that was opening in

Southampton the next day. He was busy looking up train times.

"He's supposed to be starting at John Felton on Monday, but he doesn't want to go. His mother says he had some bad experiences at his last school. I said you'd talk to him."

"Talk to him?"

"Yes. You know. Reassure him. Tell him there's nothing to worry about." Mrs. Meredith picked up a fresh brush to put in a touch of ocher for the swan's eye. "I said you'd walk to school with him on Monday. Show him around. Make sure he gets to his classes, that sort of thing."

Francis came over to stand on the step that led out to the studio. "You told someone I'd take their son to school on Monday," he said, "and look after him through the day?"

"Yes!" Mrs. Meredith smiled brightly. "He sounded very nice."

"You don't think it might have been a good idea to ask me first?"

"Why?" Mrs. Meredith put down her brush. "It's a chance to make friends with someone your own age. It's what you need!"

"How about letting me be the one who decides what I need or don't need?"

"Look, I am trying to help!" Mrs. Meredith took a deep breath. "His mother is bringing Andy around here for an hour tomorrow morning. If you don't like him, you can tell me and you need never speak to him again, but the least you can do is meet him." She held up the plate to look at the finished swan, which wasn't quite as good as she'd hoped. "And I'm quite sure, when you do, that you'll find you get on really well together."

Francis did not answer. He looked at his mother for a moment, then turned on his heel and walked out of the kitchen. Watching him go, Mrs. Meredith had the sinking feeling that it might not have been such a good idea after all.

7

If Francis was unenthusiastic about the idea of meeting the boy from number thirty-nine, Jessica, to his surprise, was even less keen.

"So we can't go to the exhibition this morning," she said, a distinctly frosty note in her voice, "because you want to be with this 'Andy' person, right?"

"I don't *want* to be with him. I *have* to. I told you. Mum's already invited him over."

"Well, I suppose if that's what Mummy said . . ."

"Oh, don't be like that!" Francis protested. "We can still go to the exhibition. Just not till this afternoon. He's only going to be here an hour!"

"One hour?" Jessica gave a sniff. "That's all?"

"Then on Monday I have to walk him to school and show him around, but after that . . ."

"You're going to spend all Monday with him as well?"

"That's why Mum wants me to meet him," said Francis patiently. "He's starting at a new school. He doesn't know anyone, and I'm supposed to help him get through the first day. After that he probably won't want to know me anyway, will he?"

"You mean when someone tells him about the dolls?"

"Yes."

Jessica considered this. Francis could tell she was still not happy.

"And what am I supposed to do while all this is going on?"

"Well, you could . . ."

"I mean, it's all right for you, isn't it? You can choose from hundreds of people who you talk to, but I can't, remember? There's only one person who even knows I exist—and you're it!" Jessica pulled up the hood of her coat. "Well, I suppose I'll see you later. If you're still interested, of course."

"I was hoping," said Francis, speaking quickly before she could disappear, "that you'd stay. At least for a bit."

"Stay? What for?"

"Well, to watch."

Jessica looked at him without speaking.

"If you stay," Francis continued, "you'll be able to see what he's like and then, when he's gone, we can talk about how awful he is."

For the first time that morning, Jessica almost smiled.

"All right," she said. "I can probably do that."

● ● ●

The meeting with Andy did not begin well. The first stumbling block was that Andy was in fact Andi—with an "i," not a "y"—and she was a girl. The figure standing at the front door was short and squat, with strong, sturdy legs, a pair of powerfully muscled arms held rigidly at her side and a head covered in short, tight curls of bright red hair. She was without doubt one of the most unattractive adolescents Mrs. Meredith had ever seen.

"Don't just stand there, Thug, darling," said her mother in a loud, deep voice. "Say hello to Mrs. Meredith."

"Thug?" said Mrs. Meredith, as a clearly reluctant Andi followed her mother into the house. "You call your daughter . . . Thug?"

"It's a nickname. Short for Thuglette." Mrs. Campion smiled fondly. "She was always getting into fights when she was little!"

"I see . . ." Mrs. Meredith smiled nervously at Andi. "Well, I'll tell Francis you're here."

As she called upstairs for her son, Mrs. Meredith already knew that the girl standing in her hallway was unlikely to have anything in common with Francis. She wasn't even sure it was safe to leave them alone together and decided it would be best if they all stayed in the kitchen, where she could keep an eye on things.

Francis appeared on the stairs.

"Hello there," boomed Mrs. Campion. "You must be Francis. This is my daughter, Andi, who might be going to the same school as you. Mightn't you, Thug?"

The Thug scowled, but did not reply.

"Well, how about you two run off upstairs and get to know each other," said Mrs. Campion, "while Grace and I have a little chat?"

"I thought perhaps we could all sit and talk together," said Mrs. Meredith, but Mrs. Campion wouldn't hear of it.

"Nonsense! Last thing two young people need is a couple of old fogies like us hanging around. Off you go!" She gave her daughter an encouraging push in the direction of the stairs. "And remember what I said!" She turned to Mrs. Meredith. "I wouldn't say no to a cup of coffee myself, though. Through here, is it?"

She was marching off toward the kitchen as she spoke, and Mrs. Meredith, with an apologetic glance at Francis, followed her.

"Okay . . ." said Francis, looking at Andi. "You want to come up?"

• • •

Francis was less worried about spending an hour with the Thug than his mother might have thought. It was not the first time she had brought home someone for him to "look after" and he had learned how to survive these encounters with minimum embarrassment.

He knew the importance of looking normal. He knew not to talk about fashion, and he knew not to show her the room at the top of the house. He could survive for an hour, even with someone like Andi.

"You've moved in down the road, have you?" he asked, as he led the way into his bedroom. "When was that?"

"Two weeks ago," said Andi.

Jessica was standing by the window as they came in. She had intended to keep quiet and not say or do anything that might distract Francis while he was looking after his visitor, but she quite forgot this when she saw Andi.

"Hey!" she said. "She's a girl!"

"Yes, I'm a girl," snapped the Thug. "You have a problem with that?"

She was staring directly at Jessica, who was too astonished to answer.

"Are you talking to me?" asked Francis.

"No. I'm talking to her!" Andi pointed directly at Jessica.

"Oh . . ." Francis's brain absorbed this information. "You mean you can see her?"

"Of course I can see her!" The Thug gave him a look of withering scorn. "Why wouldn't I see her?"

"Well, most people can't," said Francis simply. "In fact, until now, the only person who could see her was me."

"You can see all of me, can you?" asked Jessica. "Clothes, hair . . . everything?"

There was an icy look in Andi's eyes. You could tell she thought she was being made fun of, and she didn't look like the sort of girl who took being made fun of lying down. Jessica sensed that a rapid explanation was called for and stepped forward.

"The thing is, I'm dead," she explained. "So most people can't see me because I haven't really got a body." As she spoke, she ran her hand through the end of Francis's bed, her arm brushing through the wood as if it were a patch of fog.

The glare faded from the Thug's face as she stared at the bed, at the arm, and finally at Jessica's face.

"Do that again," she said.

Obligingly, Jessica put her arm through the bed and then, for good measure, took two steps sideways so that she was standing in the middle of the mattress.

There was another long pause while Andi stared some more. Then a faint smile crossed her face.

"Whooo!" She came over and stood by the bed, staring at the point where Jessica's waist disappeared into the duvet. "So what are you? Some sort of ghost?"

"Yes. I suppose I am."

"And nobody else can see her?" Andi turned to Francis.

"Not that we know of."

"And you really are, like . . . dead?"

Jessica nodded. "For about a year now."

"Oh, yes!" There was the light of real interest and enthusiasm in Andi's eyes and the smile grew wider. "That is *so* cool!"

8

Downstairs, Mrs. Meredith was becoming increasingly alarmed. Mrs. Campion had been talking about her daughter for nearly forty minutes now, and the more she said, the more fearful Mrs. Meredith became for the safety of her son.

"She's not a violent person by nature," Mrs. Campion was saying. "She's more . . . high-spirited. She grew up surrounded by boys, you see. I mean, for a long time, she thought she *was* one. Like those geese that are brought up by ducks, you know? But now she's older it's all gotten more difficult. The boys don't want her around because she's a girl, and the girls don't want her because, well, she's not very girly."

Mrs. Meredith could only agree. There had been nothing remotely girly about Andi.

"The trouble is, although she looks tough on the

outside, she's really quite sensitive. You say the wrong word and she flies off the handle, and she just doesn't know her own strength." Mrs. Campion sighed. "That's why the last school asked her to leave."

"They did?" said Mrs. Meredith.

"Personally, I thought they blew the whole thing way out of proportion." Mrs. Campion sipped at her coffee. "I mean, children break bones all the time, don't they? I thought expelling her for what was basically an accident was way over the top. But by then, of course, the other parents had organized this petition . . ."

"Ah . . ." Mrs. Meredith tried to look sympathetic, but a large part of her simply wanted to run upstairs and make sure Francis was still in one piece.

"And since she left, she's found it very difficult to settle. We've tried to get her into several schools, but this is the first one that would take her—and now she says she doesn't want to go!" Mrs. Campion stared moodily into her cup. "As if I didn't have enough on my plate already, with Peter spending nine months of the year in Kuwait, and a father with Alzheimer's . . . When you said the other day you had a boy the same age, I thought, that's perfect! If they can get to know each other, make friends, maybe . . . maybe . . ."

She stopped, and Mrs. Meredith noticed to her astonishment that a huge tear was trickling down the woman's cheek.

"Sorry about this. Making a complete idiot of myself as usual." Mrs. Campion's voice was no longer booming. "It's just there's nothing worse, is there, as a parent, than seeing your child miserable. Not knowing what to do about it." She took out a tissue and blew her nose. "I thought if she had someone to take her into school, show her around, look after her . . . and your Francis sounds like such a *nice* boy."

"He is," said Mrs. Meredith. "He's very nice. But to be honest, I'm not sure he's the sort of person to help someone like Andi."

"No? Well, I suppose it was always a long shot. I hope you don't mind my trying. You try anything when you're as desperate as I am." Mrs. Campion looked at her watch and stood up. "It might be a good idea to call them down now. I don't want to alarm you but it's best not to leave Thuglette alone with strangers for too long. You never know what might set her off."

Together the two women went out to the hall and Mrs. Meredith called up to her son that it was time for Andi to go.

Francis's face appeared over the banister.

"Already?" He looked rather disappointed.

"Why do we have to go now?" Andi's face had appeared beside Francis. "We've only just gotten here."

"We have to be at Grandad's by twelve," said Mrs. Campion briskly. "And you know how upset he gets if we're late."

"Can I come back tomorrow?" asked Andi.

Mrs. Campion looked startled. "Well, I . . . That would depend on Francis."

"It's okay with me." Francis looked at Andi. "Tomorrow's fine."

"Or you could come to my house. I've got this great room on the top floor. Really private."

"Okay." Francis nodded. "Sounds good."

Mrs. Meredith could hardly believe her ears. She wondered briefly if Andi was somehow forcing him to agree to the meeting, but Francis didn't look as if he was being forced. He looked as if it was something he wanted to do.

"About nine?" Andi was starting down the stairs. "Is that too early?"

"No. Nine's fine."

"Great." Andi smiled. "See you tomorrow, then!"

"I can't believe it." Mrs. Campion spoke in a hoarse whisper. "He's got her eating out of his hand. How did he do it?"

Mrs. Meredith had no idea. As she followed her guests to the door, she was still trying to work out what had astonished her most. The fact that her son should be setting up a meeting with someone as bizarre as Andi, or Andi's smile as she said good-bye.

She looked quite different when she smiled.

Almost like a girl.

9

The next morning, at nine o'clock, Andi answered the front door before Francis had even rung the bell, and watched admiringly as Jessica floated into the hall.

"Is that how you normally move?" she asked.

"I suppose it is," said Jessica, "unless I materialize, of course."

"Materialize?"

"That's when I think myself somewhere." To illustrate, Jessica disappeared, and then reappeared on the other side of the hall.

"Oh, that is *so* unbelievable!" Andi clapped her hands in delight. "And you can go anywhere like that?"

Jessica was explaining that she could usually only materialize to places she could see, or that were already familiar, when Mrs. Campion's voice called from the back of the house.

"Was that someone at the door, Thug?"

"It's all right!" Andi called back. "It's Francis!" She took his arm. "Come on, we'll go up to my room."

She led Francis toward the stairs but then stopped to watch, openmouthed, as Jessica's body moved effortlessly up and through the ceiling above.

"I expect this is nothing to you," she said to Francis. "You've seen it all before, right?"

Francis agreed that he had often seen Jessica float through ceilings. "You get used to it," he said.

"You might." Andi gazed admiringly at Jessica's feet as they disappeared. "I don't think I will."

• • •

Andi's room on the top floor was the same size as the one at the top of Francis's house, but mostly furnished with sports equipment. There was a rack of weights, a rowing machine, a basketball hoop on one wall, a treadmill and, under the skylight, an enormous punching bag swung gently from a hook in the ceiling.

The three of them stayed up there all morning and, for most of that time, Andi questioned Jessica on what it was like being a ghost. She wanted to know if Jessica minded being dead? What did it feel like? Did she ever eat, or get hungry? What did she see when she moved through walls? Had she met any other dead people and would she be frightened if she did? Did she think she'd be a ghost forever, and what else might happen to her if she didn't?

In the course of a couple of hours, she found out more things about Jessica's life—both before and after she had died—than Francis had discovered in a fortnight. He knew that Jessica's mother had died of a brain tumor two years before, and that Jessica had gone to live with her grandmother, but she had never told him that her grandmother had died as well, the following year, and that Jessica had then been taken in by her aunt Jo and uncle George. The two deaths, coming so closely together, Francis thought, must have been a difficult time.

Andi was particularly interested to hear that Francis was able to "feel" Jessica's hands when she touched him, and instantly wanted to experiment with it herself. She sat cross-legged on the floor and waited while Jessica thrust her hands into her shoulders.

"That is *so* spooky!" she exclaimed, as she felt the warmth of Jessica's hands moving inside her back. Then she got her to push her arms right through and out the front, so that it looked like the monster from *Alien* was bursting out of her stomach.

But the question that Andi kept coming back to, the one that seemed to intrigue her the most, was how Jessica had died.

"You really can't remember anything about it?" she asked for the fourth time that morning. "Nothing? Nothing at all?"

"Nothing," said Jessica. "Like I told you. It's all a blank."

"Have you tried to find out?"

"How can I?" said Jessica. "I'm a ghost."

Andi thought for a moment.

"We could find out for you, couldn't we?"

"How do you mean?"

"All we have to do is phone up your aunt and uncle." Andi pulled a cell phone from her pocket. "What's their number?"

"I'm not sure that's a good idea," said Francis.

"Why not?"

"Well . . ." Francis chose his words carefully. "I think if someone in my family had died and I got a phone call from a complete stranger asking how it had happened, I'd be . . . well, I'd be upset for a start, and I probably wouldn't tell them."

"Okay . . ." Andi put down the phone. "So let's think of something else."

But they were still trying to find a simple method of discovering how Jessica had died when Mrs. Campion came in to ask what they wanted for lunch.

● ● ●

Downstairs in the kitchen, while Andi had gone to the bathroom, Mrs. Campion asked Francis if he was busy that afternoon. "Only if you're not," she said, "I promised to take Thuglette ice-skating, and thought maybe you'd like to come, too."

Jessica thought ice-skating was a wonderful idea, and Francis found himself agreeing.

"Splendid!" Mrs. Campion beamed, then lowered her voice and added, "Have you managed to have a word with her yet? About school?"

"School?" said Francis.

"She's supposed to be starting tomorrow," said Mrs. Campion, "but, as I told your mother, she's been putting up a certain amount of resistance."

"Oh," said Francis. "I see."

"Anything you could say to encourage her, you know, help her get back in the swing"—Mrs. Campion looked appealingly at Francis—"would be *very* much appreciated."

Sitting down to lunch, Francis wondered how he was supposed to go about persuading someone like Andi to go to school. He wasn't even sure that he wanted to, and decided that, if Andi asked him about it, he would happily tell her anything she wanted to know, but if she didn't, he was not going to bring up the subject himself.

10

The ice-skating was more fun than Francis had expected. Andi was an experienced skater and hit the ice like a rocket, hurtling around the rink at the sort of speed that made mothers with small children move anxiously out of her way. Jessica, although she had never skated before, moved with a similar ease because, as a ghost, her skates didn't actually touch the ice. Francis at first found it difficult to stand upright, let alone move in any specific direction, and spent a lot of time clinging to the walls at the side of the rink until Andi explained the basic movements to him. By the end of an hour, however, he was getting around on his own, hardly falling over at all, and rather enjoying himself.

Andi and Jessica were brilliant together. Jessica had dressed herself in a costume she had copied from a poster she had seen on the way in, and she not only skated but did the most dramatic spins and turns before landing gracefully on one foot. She and Andi worked out a whole routine together and it was a shame, as Jessica said, that Francis was the only one who could see it. At four o'clock, when the session ended and a breathless Andi was taking off her skates, she asked what he thought they should do next.

"I'd better get home now," said Francis. "I've got some work I have to finish for school."

"Right . . ." Andi's smile faded. "I'm supposed to be going to school tomorrow as well."

"Your mum told me," said Francis. "I think I'm meant to be telling you it's a good idea."

"And is it?"

"I'm not sure." Francis frowned. "It's mostly okay. I suppose."

Andi grunted.

"What was your last school like?" asked Jessica. "We heard you didn't like it at all."

"It was a boarding school."

"Was that bad?"

Andi grimaced. "No, it was great. As long as you were tall and pretty. If you were short and ugly and looked a complete idiot in your school uniform, it was hell." She looked across at Francis. "Is that how it works at your place?"

As she spoke, Francis had a sudden picture of two of the girls in his class—Denise Ritchie and Angela Wyman. They were tall and pretty and, for reasons he had never really understood, they seemed to have the power to decide who was worth talking to and who should be ignored. As one of the people they ignored, he had never liked either of them much.

"I suppose it is," he said, "but I don't think you'd have to worry. Haven't you got a black belt in judo or something?"

"Karate," said Andi moodily, "but being able to hit people doesn't make you friends with anyone, does it? It just means you spend most of the day on your own."

"You wouldn't be on your own at Francis's school," said Jessica. "You'd have us." She looked across at Francis. "Wouldn't she?"

"Well . . ." Francis hesitated. "If she wanted . . ."

"Oh, thanks," said Andi. "That's a really reassuring vote of enthusiasm."

"I'm sorry." Francis blushed slightly. "It's just . . . if you did come to our school, you might not want to hang around with me anyway. I don't fit in very well, you see. I'm different."

"Different?" Andi frowned. "How?"

There was a long pause.

"I'd forgotten about that," said Jessica. "You'd better show her."

• • •

When they got back to Alma Road, Francis led Andi up the stairs to his room on the top floor. He watched as her eyes took in the sewing machine, the drawings on the wall, and the shelves of dolls.

"Francis made that," said Jessica, pointing at Betty, the dummy, now dressed in a completed off-white cotton shirt. "And he made all these as well." She floated over to the dolls. "They're a sort of history of fashion in the last fifty years."

Andi followed her across and picked up one of the dolls, a figure dressed mostly in studded red leather.

"You made this?" she asked.

Francis nodded.

"He did all the drawings, too." Jessica gestured to the pictures on the wall. "They're all his own designs. He's brilliant!"

"This is what makes you different?" said Andi, looking at Francis.

"Well, it's not the sort of hobby that makes you the class hero."

"Ha!" Andi gave an odd laugh. "I have an uncle who works in the fashion industry. His whole house looks like this, and he earns a fortune." She put the doll back on the shelf. "This isn't *different*. If you want to be different, try being a girl who looks so much like a boy that the teacher sends you to the wrong changing room."

"If you're talking about being different," said Jessica, "both of you should try being dead and nobody talking to you for a year."

Francis took a deep breath.

"In that case," he said slowly, "maybe we should stick together tomorrow. The three of us."

"I'll go for that," said Andi.

● ● ●

Sometime later that evening, Jessica suggested that if Andi was worried about how she looked in a school uniform, she should get Francis to help.

"How do you mean?" asked Andi.

"Well, if any of it doesn't fit properly," said Jessica, "you could get him to alter it. He's good at that sort of thing."

Andi looked doubtful.

"You should let him try," said Jessica. "Really, you should."

So Andi went home and returned a few minutes later with the uniform her mother had bought the previous week. She changed out of her jeans, put on the skirt and blazer, and examined her reflection in the mirror. It was every bit as bad as she remembered. The skirt stuck out at the sides and the back, making her look even shorter and stumpier than she already was.

"Yes . . ." Francis studied her critically. "It's the skirt we need to look at first." He walked around her several times, making marks on the gray material with a piece of chalk. "It sits all wrong. But if we rejig the side seams . . . and the hemline, of course . . . It shouldn't be too difficult."

A moment later, the skirt was laid out on the table under the skylight. He was unpicking the seams and then cutting at the separate pieces with a pair of scissors.

Standing there in her underwear, Andi watched him, a little nervously.

"You needn't worry." Jessica stood beside her. "He knows what he's doing."

And it certainly seemed that he did. They watched as, with deft fingers, he pinned the pieces back together, threaded a reel of gray cotton on to the machine, and set about sewing a new seam. In less than twenty minutes, he was handing the skirt back to her and telling her to try it on.

The result was extraordinary. It was still the same skirt, made of the same material and worn by the same person, but it no longer stuck out at the back, the length was perfect, and it looked . . . well, it looked like you'd expect a skirt to look.

"Not bad," Francis murmured. "I'll just run around the hemline and then we'll see if we've got time to do something with the blazer."

• • •

Mrs. Campion couldn't help thinking it had been a remarkably successful day. She had called round to number forty-seven to check that everything was still all right between her daughter and Francis, and then Mrs. Meredith had shown her the pottery. The plates and bowls she had produced were lovely, really lovely, and it was extraordinary to think she had a problem selling them.

Mrs. Campion had some experience of selling things. In the days before Andi was born, she had worked as the sales manager for an electrical company, and the idea that the two women should team up had occurred to them both at almost the same time. Mrs. Meredith would make her plates and bowls, and Mrs. Campion would sell them. Of course, she would have to sort out this business of getting Andi back to school first, but if things continued to go well with Francis, maybe, in a week or two . . .

Her thoughts were interrupted by the sound of the front door opening, and Mrs. Campion went out into the hall to find Andi taking her key from the lock.

"You're wearing your school uniform!" she said.

"I've been showing it to Francis," said Andi. "To make sure I'd gotten it right for tomorrow."

"Tomorrow?" Mrs. Campion could hardly believe her ears. "You're going to school tomorrow?"

"Francis says we need to leave about eight thirty." Andi was heading for the stairs. "So I need to be up by seven thirty. Okay?"

"Yes, of course." Mrs. Campion tried to keep the astonishment from her voice. "I'll give you a call!"

How on earth had Francis done it, she wondered? How on earth had he made her change her mind? More to the point, how had he turned her defiant and deeply resentful daughter into the bright and cheery girl who was climbing the stairs to her room, and all within the space of a day and a half?

It was a miracle. The whole thing was a miracle.

11

Brenda Parsons, the new principal of John Felton, was a little surprised when Francis appeared in her office on Monday morning with the request that Andi be placed in the same class as him. She had read Andi's file, and wondered if he knew what he was letting himself in for.

"Are you sure about this?" she asked. "You know, she comes here with a certain . . . reputation."

"I know," said Francis. "But we seem to get along. And I thought if we were in the same class, it might help Andi settle in."

"Yes. Well, it's a kind thought." Mrs. Parsons consulted the file on her desk. "But I'm afraid that won't be possible."

"Oh . . ." Francis looked rather crestfallen. "Why not?"

"According to Andi's file, her work is not at the same standard as yours. If she moved into your class, she'd never be able to keep up."

"I see . . ." Francis frowned. "Is it possible that there's been some sort of mistake?"

"I'm sorry?"

"It's just that when I was doing my math homework the other night," said Francis, "I got the feeling Andi would have no trouble with it. No trouble at all."

"Really?" Mrs. Parsons looked at the math report in Andi's file. It said things like "has little natural ability" and "makes no effort to fulfill her potential," which at least implied that there was a potential to fulfill. "I tell you what." She closed the file. "We'll see how it goes for a week, and if her work is as good as you say, I'll move her up a level."

"Would it be possible," said Francis, "to put her in my class to start with, and then put her *down* a class if it didn't work out?" He leaned forward in his chair. "The thing is, I think Andi was very unhappy in her last school, and that's partly why she got into trouble there. I think if she was with me, there'd be less chance of that happening. We really would like to be together if it was possible. We have . . . we have things in common."

Mrs. Parsons took off her glasses and twirled them thoughtfully between her fingers. She did not normally debate her decisions with pupils, but Francis had a point. Judging by her past record, Andi was not going to find it easy to settle in at John Felton, and being with a friend might help curb her tendency to lash out when provoked.

"All right," she said. "We'll try it your way. But if she can't cope with the work, I'll have to move her down. There's no point her being in a class where she can't understand the lessons."

"Thank you," said Francis.

"If she's outside," said Mrs. Parsons, putting her glasses back on her nose, "you can tell her the good news and send her in. I wanted a word with her anyway."

Andi sat in the chair opposite the principal and watched as Mrs. Parsons wrote busily at her desk.

"She's writing a note to your homeroom teacher," said Jessica, hovering behind the principal's chair, "to say you'll be joining the same classes as Francis."

"I'm writing a note to your homeroom teacher," said Mrs. Parsons, "to say you'll be joining the same classes as Francis." She looked up. "He argued very persuasively on your behalf and I hope he was right when he said you could cope with the work. Mr. Williams will probably want to give you a test before he lets you join his math class, but you won't mind that, I presume?"

"Tell her it'll be fine," said Jessica. "I'm good at math. I can give you the answers."

"That'll be fine," said Andi.

"Good." Mrs. Parsons folded the note and tucked it into an envelope. "In that case, you can give this to Miss Jossaume." As Andi stood up to leave, she went on, "But before you go, I want to remind you of what I said when you came in with your mother last week. If there is any repeat of the violence you showed at your last school—any repeat at all—you will be straight out the door. So no fighting, with anyone, for any reason. Is that understood?"

"No fighting," said Andi. "Understood."

• • •

The morning went well. Francis and Andi sat together for their classes, with Jessica standing between them but with her body sunk into the floor so that her head was at the same level as theirs. In math, Mr. Williams did, as Mrs. Parsons had warned, give Andi a test, to see if she could cope with the level of work. It didn't take very long.

"What's a quarter of a half?" he demanded briskly, almost before she was inside the door.

"An eighth," said Jessica.

"An eighth," said Andi.

"Nineteen times twenty?"

"Three hundred and eighty," said Jessica.

"Three hundred and eighty," said Andi.

"Okay..." Mr. Williams looked at her carefully. "Four thousand nine hundred and ninety, take away three thousand and six."

"Hang on," said Jessica, holding up a finger to indicate she was thinking.

"Hang on," said Andi, holding up a finger.

"One thousand nine hundred and eighty-four," said Jessica.

"One thousand nine hundred and eighty-four," said Andi.

"You'll do!" Mr. Williams smiled. "Welcome to the top math class!"

He told the principal in the teachers' lounge at lunch that the new arrival was clearly a sound mathematician.

"Are you sure?" said Mrs. Parsons. "The report from her last school said she had no natural talent."

"Well, I can't understand that," said Mr. Williams cheerfully. "I asked her several questions during the lesson, and what really impressed me was the way she never *rushed* to give her answer. She always thought about it for a moment first. I liked that. It's not often you get a student who's not afraid to stop and think."

"No," said Mrs. Parsons, with a rather puzzled look on her face. "No, it isn't."

After the success of the math lesson, Andi had made a similar impression on Mrs. Archer, the history teacher, and now in the lunch break Francis and Jessica were giving her a tour of the school grounds so she knew where everything was.

They were walking around the back of the gym to the science labs when they met Quentin Howard coming the other way.

"Ah!" His face lit up when he saw Francis. "If it isn't the doll-fancier himself. And look! He's found himself a real live doll!" He peered down at the diminutive Andi. "Has he started knitting you a little cardigan yet?"

What happened next happened so fast that if Francis had blinked he would have missed it. Andi took a step forward and drove the stiffened fingers of her right hand straight into Quentin's stomach. Then, even before the pain had registered on his face, her left hand chopped down with an audible thwack onto his thigh. Quentin tried to cry out, but there was no air in his lungs to make a noise. Instead, his legs gave way, his body doubled over, and Andi caught him by the arm, calling to an openmouthed Francis to take the other side.

"Give me a hand," she said, then nodded toward a low wall. "We'll sit him down over there."

Horrified, Francis did as he was told, and together they dragged the semiparalyzed Quentin over to the wall and sat him down. Andi pushed Quentin's head down between his legs.

"You're just winded," she told him calmly. "You'll be fine in a few minutes." She waited patiently until Quentin's desperate efforts to catch his breath had subsided to an asthmatic wheeze. Then she took a firm grasp of his hair, lifted his head, and brought his face to within a few inches of her own.

"Let's get one thing straight, shall we?" Her voice was still quiet, but there was no mistaking the glint in her eyes. "I don't like people being rude to me. Or to my friends. And if you *ever* do it again . . . or if I ever hear you've said something rude about me when I'm not there . . . or if I even *think* that you might have been *thinking* something rude about me—or my friend here—you'll be going home with something a lot worse than a couple of bruises. So you'd better be very careful what you say and who you say it to. Have you got that?"

Quentin nodded.

"All right." Andi let go of his head and turned to the others. "Let's go."

Francis glanced nervously around to see if anyone had been watching. "I don't think you should have done that," he said.

"He was being rude," said Andi.

"That doesn't make it okay to hit him." Francis glanced back to where Quentin was trying manfully to stand up. His leg gave way almost immediately and he fell to the ground with a small cry of pain. "Look! He can't even walk!"

"It'll wear off in a few minutes," said Andi. "He'll be fine."

"And suppose he tells someone what you did? Suppose he goes to Mrs. Parsons?"

"He might," said Andi. "But even if he does, I'd still prefer it to him thinking he can say things like that and get away with it. He knows now that if he does it again, there will be consequences."

"Yes . . ." Francis took a last look at Quentin before they set off again to the science labs. "Well, if I'm ever rude to you, I wouldn't mind a warning *before* you start hitting me. At least give me the chance to apologize first."

"You?" Andi laughed. "I'm not sure you'd know how to be rude. People like you are just . . . nice."

"You've always been nice." Jessica threaded a ghostly hand through his other arm. "Anyone can see that."

"Mum says I should try and be more like you." Andi was still talking to Francis. "She says I should learn to walk away when someone says something to annoy me. Take no notice. Ignore them. I don't know why I can't. I think I'm just made differently." She looked up at him. "But I've always envied people like you."

"Funny you should say that," said Francis, "because I've always been a bit envious of people like you."

12

That evening, Francis was up in the attic room with Jessica, working on a skirt to go with the off-white cotton blouse. He had found a length of Prince of Wales check that he thought might match it nicely, and normally would have started by sketching out some possible designs before deciding which he liked best.

With Jessica, however, none of that was necessary. If he just showed her the material and explained roughly what he had in mind, Jessica could think herself into the design, and he could see at once whether it worked or not. If he wanted to change it, he had only to ask and Jessica would imagine a different hemline, a different waist, a tighter shape, a gentle flare . . . She could, as Francis said, earn a fortune in the fashion industry, if she could just sort out this business of most people not being able to see her.

It was while he was cutting out the paper pattern for the design they had finally settled on that he said something about the incident with Quentin that morning, and how he hoped word of it would not leak out.

"Because if Mrs. Parsons gets to hear of it," he said, "she'll tell Andi to leave. I know she will. All it'll take is for Quentin to complain. Or to tell his parents."

"I don't think he'll complain," said Jessica. "He won't want everyone to know he got thumped by a girl. Especially a girl only half his size." She paused before adding thoughtfully, "One of the others might, though."

"Others?" Francis looked up from his pattern.

"Oh, of course . . ." Jessica gave a little smile. "You weren't there, were you? She did the same thing later to Denise Ritchie and Angela Wyman."

"Are you *serious*?" Francis stared at her. "Where? When?"

"In the girls' locker room. They came in when Andi was packing up her stuff at the end of class. Angela said something like, 'Look at the hair on that one, it's like a doormat,' and Denise said, 'There should be a law saying something that ugly should be covered up' and next thing they know, Andi is standing in front of them."

She had, according to Jessica, been very calm. She had not shouted or yelled. She had simply said that she had a friend who said she ought to give people a chance to apologize when they had been rude, and that this was their chance. Angela's reply had been to try and push Andi out of the way, and a second later, she was doubled up on the ground gasping for breath, just as Quentin had been. Andi then turned to Denise, who called her a name, and a moment later she was on the floor as well.

"Andi sat them both on a bench," Jessica continued, "and gave them The Talk. You know? Like she did to Quentin? She was really calm and quiet, but she told them what would happen if they were ever rude to her again. I think they got the message."

Francis listened to the story in openmouthed astonishment. "She got into two fights? On her first day? After everything Mrs. Parsons said?"

"Yes. I know it was wrong and she shouldn't have, but . . ." Jessica's face broke into a grin. "It was *brilliant*!"

● ● ●

Francis may not have approved of what Andi had done, but the results, in the short term, at least, were surprisingly pleasant.

Although neither the girls nor Quentin reported what had happened, somehow word got around very quickly among the other students that Andi was not someone you upset if you could help it. The next day, Francis noticed that people were very careful what they said when they were near her. Most of them tried not to be near her at all.

Denise and Angela in particular made sure they kept out of her way. In the weeks that followed, neither of them ever spoke to her or about her to anyone else. It was almost as if they had decided to pretend she did not exist.

And with Quentin, the results were even more dramatic. If they passed him in the corridor, he would avoid any eye contact, and hurry past as quickly as he could. In the science class they shared, he sat as far away from Francis and Andi as possible, and there was never a hint of the once regular jokes about what clothes Francis might be making for his dolls these days.

The difference this made to Francis's life at school was extraordinary. He still did not really approve of what Andi had done, but being able to go through the day without wondering when Quentin might appear and what he would say when he did was like a huge weight lifted from his shoulders. He had had to brace himself, mentally, against it for so long that he had almost forgotten how good it was not to have to worry about what people might say. Because now, nobody said anything.

They didn't dare.

• • •

As a sort of thank-you present, Francis made Andi a T-shirt. It was in red, her favorite color, with a design on the front that was slightly off beat—and she liked it. She liked it so much that she asked him to make her another one, so she would still have one to wear while the other was being washed. He did as she asked and, a little later, made her a sort of vest out of some denim material that went with it rather well, and she liked that, too.

Mrs. Campion saw it, and was most impressed.

"Does he do all this sewing himself?" she asked Mrs. Meredith when they were sitting one day in the kitchen. "Or do you help him?"

Mrs. Meredith laughed. "I'm not allowed anywhere near his precious sewing machine," she said. "I'm far too clumsy." She held out the check that Mrs. Campion had just given her. "Look, are you sure this is all mine? It seems rather a lot for a few bowls."

"That is just the beginning," said Mrs. Campion happily. "I promise you, by the time I'm finished you'll be needing to take on extra help." She sipped thoughtfully at her coffee. "It's funny, isn't it?"

"What is?"

"How the two of them get on together. I mean, Thuglette's never been remotely interested in fashion, and Francis doesn't seem to like sports . . ." Mrs. Campion paused. "Yet they seem to spend all their time together. Do you have any idea what they talk about?"

"Not really," said Mrs. Meredith. "They come back in from school, disappear upstairs, and that's virtually all I see of them."

"Yes." Mrs. Campion nodded. "That's what happens when they come to me as well."

At that moment the front door opened and Francis called from the hall to say that he and Andi were going upstairs. It was something that seemed to involve a lot of laughing and noise.

"Still," said Mrs. Campion, as the noise receded, "I'm not complaining. They sound happy enough."

Andi and Francis *were* happy, though they would both have found it difficult to explain why. It wasn't as if they did anything very much. Mostly they were just hanging out together. They went to school, they came home, they did homework, Andi worked out, Francis made things or drew them . . .

But they had Jessica and, as Andi said, almost anything was fun when you did it with a ghost for company. Watching Jessica think herself into a new outfit—which she did several times a day—could make clothes interesting even to Andi. Sitting in class with someone who might suddenly decide to pose on the teacher's desk in a bikini could make any lesson amusing, while a walk into town with someone who could walk through walls and tell you what was going on on the other side was never going to be dull. Andi figured you'd have to be dead not to enjoy life with someone like Jessica around.

But there was one thing that bothered her. She still had no answer to the question she had asked Jessica that first weekend. The question of how Jessica had died. Neither Jessica nor Francis seemed to have much interest in the subject themselves, but Andi had never lost her desire to find the answer and she had worked out a very simple way it could be done. If the others weren't interested, she decided, then she would do it alone.

Because it was the sort of thing Jessica *ought* to know.

Everyone should know how they had died.

13

Andi's plan, which she outlined on the walk to school, was to go out to the village where Jessica used to live.

"What for?" asked Francis. "You can't knock on her aunt's door and ask what happened. That'd be just as bad as phoning."

"We don't have to knock on anyone's door," said Andi patiently. "We just have to ask at the shop."

"The shop?"

"There was a shop in the village where you lived, wasn't there?" Andi turned to Jessica. "And they know everything in the village shop. All I'll have to do is walk in and say, 'I used to know someone called Jessica Fry, have you heard what happened to her?' and they'll tell me." She paused. "I thought we could go out there this weekend."

Jessica said she couldn't see the point. She had never

been interested in finding out why she had died. It had never seemed important. There were, she said, much more exciting things they could do.

Andi, however, persisted.

"You might not be interested, but *I* am," she said. "And it'll give you a chance to look around where you used to live. See if anything's changed. Maybe look in the churchyard to see if you've got a gravestone—you *have* to be interested in that!"

Jessica pointed out that, if she had been interested, she could probably have done all those things already, but Andi was not deterred. It would only take an hour or so, she argued. She had told her mother that Francis wanted to visit a friend's grave and Mrs. Campion had already agreed to take them. Jessica didn't *have* to come with them, but it would be *so* much more fun if she did . . .

Andi could be very single-minded when she had set her heart on something, and none of them was really surprised when, that Saturday afternoon, they were all to be found in Mrs. Campion's car while she drove them the seven miles to the village where Jessica had lived.

● ● ●

Parking her car outside the church, Andi's mother told Francis he could take as long as he liked because she had plenty of phone calls to make. So while Andi walked off to find the shop, he pushed open the gate to the churchyard and went inside, with Jessica floating beside him.

It didn't take long to find the grave. All the new burials were together in the same section, and one of them was marked by a small square stone, laid flat in the grass. Written on it were Jessica's name, the year she had been born, the year she died, and the words DEEPLY LOVED. Around it someone had planted a circle of primroses that were just coming into flower. Looking at it gave Jessica an odd sensation.

"So where did you live?" Francis asked.

"What?"

"Your house. Was it near here?"

"It was over there." Jessica pointed across the tombstones to a group of houses, just visible through the trees on the other side of the road. "Bannock Lane. We were the last house on the right."

As she said it, Jessica's mind filled with pictures—of her room over the front hall, of sitting in the living room watching television with her aunt and uncle, of eating meals around the little table in the kitchen.

"Perhaps I *will* go and take a look at it," she said. "Do you mind?"

"Course not," said Francis. "I'll wait here."

"Thanks." Jessica was already floating toward the road, her feet stroking the grass as she went. "I'll only be a couple of minutes."

● ● ●

The house was exactly as she remembered. As she stepped through the front door into the hallway, she found the same patterned wallpaper, the same carpet, the same coat hooks on the paneled wood to the right, even the same coats. There was one difference, though. On the wall to her left, opposite the living room, was a large picture of herself. It was a copy of her last school photo, and seeing her own face smiling out gave her the same odd feeling as looking at the gravestone.

Jessica wandered through to the sitting room, where she noticed the television had been replaced, then to the dining room, which was full of Uncle George's files and business reports as always, and then through to the kitchen. Nothing had changed. The bread bin, the sugar bowl, the kettle . . . everything was exactly as she remembered. She stared out of the window at the back-yard for a moment, and then went back out to the hall and up the stairs.

The first room at the top was the bathroom, Aunt Jo and Uncle George's bedroom was to the right, the spare room was to the left, and along the landing was the room at the front of the house that had been hers. The door was shut and, as Jessica stepped through it, she was shocked to discover that this room had changed completely.

Everything she remembered had gone. The bed, the wardrobe, the little cabinet with her collection of drag-ons, the bookshelves, the television, even the carpet and curtains—had all been stripped away. The room had been repainted, and a fancy new desk ran along the wall under the window, with a new computer, a tele-phone, a printer, and a swivel chair. The wall to her right, where her bed had been, was taken up with shelves containing piles of papers, magazines, and a large, three-drawer filing cabinet.

Her aunt and uncle must have taken over the space to carry on some part of their business, and the only thing left of Jessica was a collage that hung on the wall behind the door. It was made from dozens of photographs of her, all glued onto a large piece of card under a glass sheet. There were pictures of her as a baby with her parents, then as a toddler living with her mother, then of her and her grandmother and, along the bottom, more pictures from the months she had lived with her uncle and aunt. Jessica had never seen half of them before, and she stared at them for several minutes, trying to work out where they had been taken. She was still staring when she heard the sound of someone opening the front door.

She waited as whoever had come in walked briefly through to the kitchen, then came back into the hall and up the stairs. She listened as they walked along the landing, the door opened . . .

And Aunt Jo came into the room.

• • •

"Where's she gone?" asked Andi when she arrived at the churchyard and found Francis on his own.

"She went to look at her old house," said Francis. "What did you find out?"

"Nothing." Andi shook her head. "The people in the shop are new and they'd never heard of Jessica." She stamped her feet to keep warm in a breeze that was turning chilly. "Is she going to be long?"

"I don't think so," said Francis. "She said just a few minutes."

But Jessica was not back in a few minutes. Nor was she back in twenty.

"Do you think your mum would mind if I walked round to the house," said Francis, "to see if anything's wrong?"

"You think something's wrong?"

"Yes," said Francis. He had no idea why, but he did.

Mrs. Campion said she didn't mind waiting—she was working her way down a long list of phone calls—and Andi said she would stay by the car while Francis walked across to Bannock Lane. When he got to the last house on the right, he stared up at the semi-detached stone-fronted building, with its neat yard and a garage to one side, wondering what to do next. There was no sign of Jessica. He peered over the fence at the windows to try to see her inside, but she wasn't there.

He thought about knocking on the door in case she was in trouble and needed help, but then realized that if anyone answered, he could hardly ask if they had a ghost inside. And if no one answered, what was the point of knocking? He was still wondering what to do when the front door opened and a woman appeared. She was tall, with short black hair, and she walked down the path toward him.

"Hello," she said. "Is everything all right?"

"Yes, thank you," said Francis. "I'm . . . waiting for a friend."

"I see." The woman nodded. "You want to talk while you wait?"

"No. No, it's all right." Francis backed away. "I'm fine."

"Okay." The woman reached into the pocket of her skirt, took out a card, and passed it across. "Perhaps you'd like to take this. In case you change your mind."

Francis took the card. It had *Joanna Barfield— Counselor* written on it, with a telephone number and an email address underneath.

"Did you . . . did you know someone called Jessica Fry?" asked Francis.

The woman was already heading back up the path to the house, but she stopped and turned.

"Yes. She was my niece. She died just over a year ago. Did you know her?"

Francis wasn't quite sure how to answer that.

"I'd heard of her," he said.

The woman nodded, then pointed at the card. "You can call that number any time," she said. "Any time at all."

14

When Francis got back to the car, Mrs. Campion was still sitting in the driver's seat, her phone glued to one ear, while Andi was leaning against the hood, waiting for him.

"Did you find the house?" she asked.

"Yes."

"And Jessica?"

Francis shook his head.

"So what do we do?"

"I suppose we . . . go home."

"And leave her behind?"

"It's not like she'll be stranded," said Francis. "All she has to do is close her eyes and think herself back. She might have done it already."

But when they got back to Alma Road, there was no sign of Jessica. She was not at Francis's house, nor at

Andi's. She did not appear that evening and there was no sign of her the following day.

Nor the day after.

Nor the day after that.

● ● ●

It was not an easy time.

The friend with whom Francis had shared almost every waking hour for the last month had vanished out of his life, and he had no idea where she had gone or why. She had disappeared as suddenly and unexpectedly as she had appeared that first day on the playing field. And he missed her.

Andi missed her as well, and they both found her disappearance difficult to accept. They stayed very close to each other in the days that followed, talking endlessly about what might have happened, where Jessica might have gone, and when she might come back. But the simple truth was that neither of them had the least idea.

On Monday evening, after a rather gloomy day in school, they were up in the attic room, where Andi was trying on the off-white cotton blouse that Francis had been altering to fit her. Altering the blouse and the

Prince of Wales check skirt to fit Andi had been Jessica's idea—she had said it was wasted sitting on Betty the dummy—and it was while Francis was marking up the alterations that he suddenly realized Andi was crying.

"It's all my fault, isn't it?" she said, the tears trickling down her cheeks. "If I hadn't made her go out to the village with us, all this would never have happened. She'd still be here, wouldn't she?"

"We don't know that anything *has* happened." Francis reached out to take the blouse before Andi could use the sleeve to wipe her nose. "It may be something ghosts do every once in a while. We'll have to ask her about it when she comes back."

"But what if she never comes back? What if she's gone for good and we never see her again?"

"We'll see her again," said Francis firmly. "I know we will."

"You know?"

"Yes," said Francis. "I don't know how I know. But I know."

And there was indeed something deep in Francis that told him the story was not over yet, and that Jessica would be back.

Even so, it was a huge relief when she appeared in his bedroom while he was getting dressed for school on Wednesday morning.

• • •

She was wearing a hospital gown—nothing else, not even shoes—and had a slightly dazed look. Not that Francis was bothered. He was just overwhelmingly pleased to see her.

"Thank goodness!" he said. "Where have you been? Are you all right?"

"I think so." Jessica had the look of someone who's been knocked down by a car and still hasn't quite recovered.

"So what happened?"

Jessica had, it turned out, no idea where she had been or what had happened. All she knew was that she had found herself in the little room on the third floor at the hospital that morning feeling, as she described it, "sort of strange"—and not even sure what day it was.

"I checked the calendar on the nurse's desk," she said, "which said it was Wednesday, then realized I couldn't remember Monday or Tuesday." She frowned. "Last time I saw you was Saturday, right?"

"We went out to where you used to live," said Francis. "In the afternoon."

"Did we?" Jessica looked puzzled.

"We went to the graveyard and then you went over to your aunt's house and never came back. You don't remember?"

"Oh . . ." Jessica nodded. "Yes, I do. A bit."

"Did something happen at the house?"

Jessica opened her mouth to answer . . . and disappeared again.

This time, fortunately, she was not gone for long, and twenty minutes later she popped up between Francis and Andi, still wearing the hospital gown, as they were walking to school.

"What happened?" she said.

"You disappeared again," Francis told her.

"Again?" Jessica frowned. "Why do I keep doing that?"

"We don't know," said Andi, "but I wish you'd stop. It's very upsetting."

"And you need to get changed into proper clothes," said Francis. "You're all hanging out at the back."

"Oh, right . . ." Jessica concentrated for a moment and the hospital gown was replaced by jeans and a coat. "Better?"

"Much better." Andi smiled. "You really have no idea why you disappeared?"

"No." Jessica shook her head. "Not a clue."

When she disappeared twice more in the course of the morning, however, a part of the reason soon became clear. On each occasion, she disappeared when Francis or Andi asked questions about what had happened during the visit to her aunt's house on Saturday.

They decided very quickly that there must be no more talk of aunts, houses, the village, or whatever had happened that day. There must be no more investigations, either, into Jessica's past. Interesting though it might be to find out why she had died, if it was going to make her disappear, it simply wasn't worth the risk. Life with Jessica's ghost was too good to do anything that might mean losing her.

Especially, as Andi said, with a math test coming up on Friday.

• • •

The sight of their contented children was an unceasing marvel to both Mrs. Campion and Mrs. Meredith. Mrs. Meredith saw with relief how Francis had lost that downtrodden, slightly hunted look that had worried her for so long, while the change in Andi was some-thing Mrs. Campion still found hard to believe. Everything about her daughter seemed to have been transformed. She was getting good reports from school, she'd stopped hitting people, she even dressed differ-ently—something Mrs. Campion found particularly puzzling.

Andi had never been interested in clothes—out of school, she had simply worn the same jeans and T-shirt every day until they disintegrated—but in the last few weeks that had changed. It had begun with the T-shirts Francis had made her, then she had asked for money to buy new clothes in town, and now, when Mrs. Campion had asked her to find something nice to wear when they went up to London, she had appeared in an off-white cotton top and a very fetching little skirt in a Prince of Wales check that fit her like a dream. Mrs. Campion almost cried when she saw it. Her little Thuglette! In a proper skirt!

How all these changes had come about she did not know, but Mrs. Campion was certain of one thing. The person responsible was Francis. She did not know *how* he had done it but, in her eyes, the boy from number forty-seven had the status of something close to a god.

She told anyone and everyone the incredible story as often as she could. She told them how her daughter had refused point-blank to go to school, how she met Francis, and how within a day he had not only persuaded her to go to school, but to knuckle down to do some work while she was there.

"I've no idea how he did it," she would say in her booming voice, "and I've never dared to ask, but I'll tell you something. That is the most remarkable boy I've ever met. Absolutely. No question. The *most* remarkable boy."

She repeated the story as often as she could to anyone who would listen, which led to what was, in many ways, the strangest part of this story.

15

"I had a phone call last night from someone called Angela Boyle," said Mrs. Meredith at breakfast, "asking if you could help."

"Help with what?" said Francis.

"She's got a son called Roland, who goes to St. Saviour's, but a month ago, he said he didn't want to go anymore. She was hoping you could make him change his mind."

"Me?" said Francis. "What am I supposed to do?"

"She wants you to talk to him. Like you did to Andi. I told her you'd come over some time this morning."

Francis sighed. One day, he thought, he must have a serious talk with his mother about boundaries.

"You weren't doing anything else, were you?"

It was a Saturday, and Andi had gone to London to see her father, who was over from Kuwait for twenty-four hours. The fact that Francis had been planning a day of window-shopping with Jessica was not something he could explain to his mother.

"I don't see how I can persuade someone I don't know to go to school."

"All you have to do is talk to him." Mrs. Meredith poured herself another cup of coffee. "They live in one of those big houses on Paterson Road. It won't take you long to bike there, and if it doesn't work you can come straight home again. Think of it as your good deed for the day."

Reluctantly, Francis agreed.

"Though the whole thing's completely pointless," he told Jessica when she appeared, half an hour later. "I mean, what can I say that would make a complete stranger decide to go back to school when he doesn't want to?"

"Nothing," said Jessica, imagining herself into a pair of gloves and a cashmere scarf. "So it won't take very long, will it?"

In fact, it took longer than either of them had expected. To start with, Francis had a flat tire, which took twenty minutes to change, and then he found the house was right at the far end of Paterson Road, which meant cycling almost another mile and a half. By the time he arrived, hot and sweating, he was not in the mood to help anybody, but he left his bike on the gravel in front of one of the largest houses he had ever seen, and rang the front doorbell.

"I'll go in and take a look around," said Jessica. "See you in a minute, okay?"

Francis nodded, and waited on the porch until Mrs. Boyle answered the door. She was a small, worried-looking woman, nervously twisting a handkerchief between her fingers.

"This is so kind of you, Francis," she said, when he had introduced himself. "You've heard about Roland's little problem, have you?"

"Mum said he didn't want to go to school."

"That's right." Mrs. Boyle blushed. "We're not expecting miracles, of course, but if you could talk to him and find out what's wrong. Maybe get him to . . ." She hesitated. "Frieda Campion said you'd done these extraordinary things for her daughter and if you were able to do anything like that for Rollo . . ."

"I'll talk to him," said Francis, "but if he doesn't want to go to school, I don't think it'll do any good."

"No. No, possibly not"—Mrs. Boyle's handkerchief

twisting intensified—"but I'm *so* grateful to you for try-ing." She lifted her head and bellowed down the hall with surprising force. "Roland! Your friend's here!" She turned back to Francis. "I've told him you're coming and he's really looking forward to it. Roland!" She shouted again. "Roland! Come and say hello!"

They waited for some time but there was no sign of Roland, and eventually Mrs. Boyle took Francis down the hall and along a passageway to his room, where she knocked timidly at the door.

"Are you there, dear?" she asked. "It's your friend Francis come to see you. I told you about him, remember?"

Still no answer.

"Perhaps you could go in on your own," whispered Mrs. Boyle. "He's been a bit moody recently, but I know he wants to see you really."

Francis pushed open the door and went inside.

The curtains were tightly drawn and the only light in the room came from a computer screen in one cor-ner, showing two zombies advancing toward a man who was holding a chainsaw. As his eyes adjusted to the darkness, Francis could make out an unmade bed against one wall, a floor littered with clothes and empty cans of soda, a table covered in plates of half-eaten food, and a wide-screen television hanging on one of the walls.

Roland himself was sitting in front of the computer, and he was . . . large. Sitting in a swivel chair that groaned under his weight when he moved, the flesh at the sides of his body spilled over the armrests. Francis had never seen anyone so big.

Roland seemed quite unaware that anyone had entered the room, and continued tapping at his keyboard.

"Hi," said Francis.

The tapping did not stop. The man with the chainsaw had used it to lop off the heads of the zombies, but there were four more emerging from a ruined graveyard and Roland continued to sit there, playing his game. Francis felt a surge of irritation. He had better things to do with his time than stand in a darkened room being ignored by someone he hadn't wanted to meet in the first place.

"Right," he said. "I take it you *don't* want to see me, and that's fine. But next time you might try *telling* someone before I waste half my morning biking over here."

He turned on his heel, then walked back out the door and along the passageway to the front hall. He supposed he ought to say good-bye to Mrs. Boyle but there was no sign of her and, frankly, he didn't care. He left, not even bothering to close the front door behind him.

Jessica appeared in the driveway.

"This is a fantastic house! You know they have an indoor swimming pool in the back? And the yard is . . ." She stopped. "What's wrong?"

"He wouldn't talk to me," said Francis. "Just sat there playing on his computer. Ignored me completely." He picked up his bike and began wheeling it toward the road. "I knew this was a waste of time."

"Hang on a minute," said Jessica. She was pointing back to the front door, where Roland had emerged, panting slightly, his eyes blinking in the unaccustomed sunlight.

"I'm sorry," he said. "You're right. I was very rude and . . ." He paused to catch his breath. "Look . . . um . . . do you want to come in and play a game or something?"

"No, thank you," said Francis. "I've had enough for one day." He continued walking down the drive.

"How about tomorrow?" Roland called after him, but Francis didn't answer.

"Your friend can come, too, if she likes."

Francis's foot froze in midstride.

"My friend?"

Roland pointed to Jessica. "You'd both be more than welcome. And I really am very sorry."

There was a long pause.

"You're inviting me as well?" said Jessica.

"Sure." Roland nodded. "If you like."

"Okay . . ." Francis gave a long sigh. "I suppose we'd better all go inside and have a talk."

16

Roland did not take the news that Jessica was a ghost as calmly as Andi had. When they got back to his room and Jessica did her demonstration of walking through furniture, he fainted. There was a lot of him to faint and he landed on the floor with enough noise to bring Mrs. Boyle scurrying down the passageway to ask rather nervously if everything was all right.

"It's okay," Francis called through the door. "Roland fell over but he's fine." He knelt down by the quivering mass on the floor that had at least opened its eyes. "You are fine, aren't you?"

"Yeah . . . Yeah, I'm okay, Mum," said Roland. His eyes were wide and large as he stared at Jessica, who was tactfully keeping herself to the other side of the room. However, as he slowly absorbed the fact that, apart from being dead, she was a perfectly ordinary girl, his fear turned to a keen interest.

He sat in his chair, listening intently, as Francis and Jessica told him the story of how she had woken up at the hospital, wandered alone for over a year, and then discovered, a few weeks before, that first Francis and then Andi were able to see and talk to her.

When the story was finally told, right up to the time Francis had biked out to Paterson Road, Roland leaned back in his chair with his hands linked together across his stomach—they only just reached—and said, "It's an interesting problem, isn't it?"

"Problem?" said Francis. He had never thought of Jessica as a problem.

"I'm sorry, I didn't mean to be rude." Roland smiled apologetically at Jessica. "But you're not supposed to be here, are you?"

"Aren't I?"

"Dead people aren't supposed to stay around on Earth," said Roland firmly. "When you die, you're supposed to move on. That's what you were expecting to do, wasn't it? At the hospital? When you said you had the feeling someone should come and tell you what to do next, but nobody did?"

Jessica nodded.

"And that'll be why you go back there each night," Roland went on, "because you're waiting to be told how to move on, but you can't. You're stuck here. That's what ghosts are, of course. Spirits that are supposed to move on, but can't."

"How do you know all this?" asked Francis.

"Well, I don't really *know* it," Roland admitted. "I'm only telling you what I've read. But it's in all the books." He gestured to the bookshelves behind him.

It turned out that most of Roland's books were about ghosts—or vampires, voodoo, black magic, possession, or the undead. He had read a good deal on the subject, and Francis was about to ask what else he knew when Mrs. Boyle knocked on the door and asked if anyone wanted lunch.

● ● ●

Roland's mother had gone to some pains to prepare a meal that the two boys might enjoy. The kitchen table— which was bigger than some of the rooms at Francis's house—was piled with plates of sausages, garlic bread, pieces of pizza, fried chicken, slices of pie, cheeses, and hams. It was, as Jessica said, enough to make even a ghost wish he or she had a body. Watching the amount Roland tucked away gave some explanation of his size, but if it worried Mrs. Boyle, she gave no sign of it. Then, when Francis felt he really couldn't eat another thing, she cleared the table and produced a couple of large fruit tarts, a bowl of trifle, and two tubs of chocolate fudge ice cream.

"I don't know if you can stay, Francis," she said as she laid the bowls and spoons on the table, "but I've turned up the heat in the pool in case either of you wanted a swim this afternoon."

The indoor swimming pool was as large as everything else in Roland's house. It had a glass ceiling, a diving board at one end, and steps leading down into the water at the other. Through a door by the shallow end, there was a changing room with whole shelves full of towels and spare swimsuits, and the water was so warm Francis could see steam rising from its surface.

He and Roland lay on sun loungers—they knew it wasn't safe to swim right after a heavy meal—and watched while Jessica swam. She moved through the water as easily as she could move through walls and doors—and could make her suit change color while she was doing it. As they watched, it occurred to Francis that Roland might be able to answer the question that Jessica had asked the first day they met.

"We've sometimes wondered," he said, "why Andi and I were the only people who could see Jessica. Andi thought maybe it was because we were psychic, but we weren't sure."

"You could be," Roland admitted, "but I don't think so."

"No?"

"In all the books I've read, psychics usually show signs of their power when they're very young, and you said nothing like this had ever happened to you or Andi before." Roland paused before adding, "And it's certainly never happened to me."

"So what do you think it is?"

"The only thing I can think of is that we're supposed to help her in some way," said Roland. "Like I told you, she's not supposed to be here, so maybe it's our job to help her get to wherever she *is* meant to be."

"Oh," said Francis. "How would we do that?"

"I've no idea." Roland shifted on his sun lounger, which creaked alarmingly. "There's a woman in Australia I talk to on the Internet about this sort of thing . . ." He glanced at his watch. "She'll be asleep at the moment, but she usually comes online about two or three in the morning. I'd like to ask her what she thinks. Would that be all right?"

"I guess," said Francis. "Though, to be honest, I don't want Jessica to go anywhere."

"You don't?"

"No," said Francis. "I like having her here."

In the pool, Jessica was doing little dolphin dives, in and out of the water, while making her bikini flash through all the separate colors of the rainbow. The two boys watched her for a moment.

"Yes." Roland nodded. "I can understand that."

Half an hour later, they went into the pool themselves, and Roland turned out to be a very competent swimmer. He might be slow and clumsy on land, but in the water he moved with the casual confidence of a walrus. For more than an hour they played, throwing a ball, diving, snorkeling—and then Mrs. Boyle came in wheeling a tea cart containing a plate of scones, some buttered crumpets, and a large chocolate cake, in case they were hungry after all that exercise.

"You don't seem to have had any trouble getting him to talk," she said to Francis as he climbed out of the water.

"No, not really."

"I wish I knew your secret!" Mrs. Boyle picked up a napkin and began twisting it. "Has he said anything about school yet?"

"Ah." Francis had quite forgotten that this was why he had originally been invited. "No. Not yet. I thought I'd leave talking about school till we got to know each other a bit."

Mrs. Boyle nodded, deeply impressed. This was undoubtedly the sort of sophisticated thinking that had led to his success with Frieda Campion's girl.

"So you're going to see him again?"

"Oh, yes." Francis nodded. "He's coming to my house tomorrow, if that's all right. I've got a friend I'd like him to meet."

Another friend! The napkin in Mrs. Boyle's fingers was twisted as tight as a wire hawser. How did he do it! Roland had refused to speak to anyone for over a fort-night and barely came out of his room for meals. Yet Francis had walked straight into the house, gotten him talking, gotten him into the pool, and now he'd arranged for him to meet someone else the following day!

Frieda Campion was right, she thought. Francis Meredith was clearly a most remarkable young man.

17

At ten o'clock the next morning, when Mrs. Meredith answered the front door, she found Roland on the step, leaning against the doorframe, breathing heavily and with the sweat dripping from his face. It was some seconds before he was able to speak.

"Name's Roland . . ." he said, when he eventually caught his breath. "Come to see . . . Francis . . ."

Mrs. Meredith brought him inside and sat him at the bottom of the stairs. She called up to Francis and then went into the kitchen to get a glass of water. By the time she returned, she was relieved to see Roland's color was a little closer to normal and she got Francis to wheel his bicycle around the back before returning to her work.

"Mum's car had to go in for a repair this morning," said Roland, when Francis returned. "So I had to bike over." He stood up to remove a backpack. "Is Jessica here?"

"She's upstairs with Andi," said Francis. "We've been waiting for you."

"Upstairs?" Roland lifted his gaze to the long flight stretching up from the hall and paled slightly.

"My room's in the attic," Francis explained apologetically. "I could get them to come down if you'd rather."

"No, no." Roland was still gazing upward. "Upstairs is good. It's best if we talk where no one can overhear."

Francis reached for the backpack. "I'll take that for you."

"Thanks," said Roland and, with a determined look, he set off.

He made it to the top with only a couple of short stops on the way, and Francis led him into the attic room, where Jessica gave him a welcoming smile.

"And this is Andi," said Francis.

"Hi," said Andi. "Did you find out?"

"Sorry?" Roland blinked at her, nervously.

"Francis said you were going to talk to someone and find out why Jessica was stuck as a ghost," said Andi. "Did you?"

"Oh . . . yes!" Roland was still breathing heavily. "Well, possibly. Do you mind if I sit down?" Without waiting for an answer, he sank gratefully onto the sofa.

Francis put the backpack on the floor beside him.

"So what did she say? Your friend?"

"Well, several things, really . . ." Roland shifted his weight to make himself comfortable. "She started by saying what I was telling you yesterday. That all ghosts are spirits that are stuck here for some reason. They're supposed to have moved on, but they can't."

"Did she say why?" Jessica had floated around to sit in the air opposite him.

"Sort of," said Roland. "She said when people die, the first thing they have to do is look at all the things they did in their lives—the things they did wrong, the things they did right—everything."

Jessica frowned. "I don't remember doing that."

"No . . ." said Roland. "And that's the point, really. You see, when you look at your life, you have to accept it. Whatever happened, you have to accept it before you can move on. And what happens to some people is, there's something they can't accept."

"Why not?" asked Francis.

"She says it's usually either because something terrible was done to them—something so awful that they don't want to see it or think about it . . ."

"Or?"

"Or it's something terrible they did themselves."

Nobody looked directly at Jessica, but you could tell what they were thinking. What could she possibly have done, or had done to her, that was so awful she couldn't even bear to think about it?

Jessica herself looked more puzzled than worried.

"I don't remember doing anything terrible," she said. "Or anyone doing anything terrible to me."

"No," said Roland, "but . . . you don't remember everything, do you?"

There was a long pause.

"You mean how I died?" said Jessica.

Roland nodded.

"The last time we tried to find out how Jessica died," said Andi, "she disappeared."

"That was because she didn't really want to know," said Roland. "My friend says if she decided—really decided—that she wanted to remember, then she would."

"No, I wouldn't!" said Jessica, crossly. "I can't choose what I remember! Either you remember something or you don't. And I don't. I don't remember how I died, I'm sorry!"

"I could tell you," said Roland. "If you like."

There was another long pause.

"You *know*?" asked Francis. "You know how she died?"

"While I was online last night . . ." Roland reached for his backpack and pulled it on to his lap. ". . . I thought I'd put Jessica's name into a couple of search engines and see what came up." He pulled out an expensive-looking laptop. "There's two newspaper articles about her, and quite a lot of stuff on a website made by her aunt." He looked at Jessica. "If you want, I could show them to you. But only if you want, obviously."

There was a silence while everyone waited for Jessica to say whether or not she wanted to see the pages on Roland's computer. But she didn't. She didn't say anything at all.

After what seemed like a very long time, she stood up.

"I need to think about this," she said. "I'm not disappearing or anything, but I need to think about this on my own."

And she disappeared.

Roland turned to Francis. "I'm sorry if all that was a bit sudden," he said, "but my friend said I had to do it. She said Jessica has to remember sometime, or she'll just stay as a ghost forever." He leaned back and looked around the room, taking in for the first time the drawings on the wall, the piles of material, and the rows of dolls.

"What's with all the dress designs and the dolls?" he asked.

"They're mine," said Francis. "It's a hobby."

"You make dresses? As a hobby?"

"Do you have a problem with that?" There was a steely look in Andi's eye as she spoke.

"No, no," said Roland hastily. "I just thought . . ." He leaned across to Francis. "Don't they give you a bit of a hard time about it at school?"

18

When Jessica reappeared, twenty minutes later, she was wearing a hospital gown. Twice in the time Francis had known her, his friend had appeared in the gown, and on both occasions it had been because her mind was concentrating on something else. The hospital gown, he knew, was like the default setting on a computer. It was what she wore if her mind was too busy to think herself into ordinary clothes.

"All right," she said. "I've decided."

Roland looked at her carefully. "And . . . ?"

"And I want to know."

"Are you sure?" asked Francis.

"Positive." Jessica looked very determined. "If Roland's right, I've got to know sometime anyway, haven't I?"

"It doesn't have to be now . . ."

"It might as well be." Jessica turned to face Roland and took a deep breath. "Okay. You can tell me. How did I die?"

"You killed yourself," said Roland. "You committed suicide."

Nobody spoke. Nobody moved. The silence in the room was so thick that it was difficult to breathe. For a moment Jessica's ghost body shimmered and dimmed, but then flickered back to normal.

"Is that true?" asked Francis quietly. "Is that what happened?"

"Mm?" Jessica turned to him. "Oh . . . yes . . . Yes, it is."

"And you remember it?"

Jessica nodded. She remembered everything now. All the days of preparation and planning, the weeks it had taken to get together enough pills, then the waiting for a time when both her aunt and uncle would be out, and the walking out into the woods at the back of the house . . .

"Why?" It was Andi who asked the question. "Why would you want to kill yourself?"

Jessica didn't answer. She was staring into the distance, lost in thought.

"Was it your aunt and uncle?" asked Francis. "Were they . . . doing something to you?"

"No, no, it wasn't anything like that," said Jessica. "They were nice. Everyone was always . . . very nice."

She could remember how nice everyone had been that day her mother had collapsed and died in the kitchen from a brain tumor. Her grandmother had been particularly nice. She had taken Jessica in and looked after her and then, when she had died of cancer a year later, everyone had been nice all over again.

Aunt Jo and Uncle George had been nice enough to say she could come and live with them and they had come to collect her and packed up all her things and been as nice as they knew how . . . But by then, of course, she was in The Pit, and when you were in The Pit, people being nice to you didn't mean anything. Nothing did.

"It's funny, isn't it," said Roland, "how people being nice doesn't help when you feel like that. You know they *want* to help, you know they're *trying* to help, but it's like they're in another world. They have no idea how you're really feeling. Or what to do about it."

Yes, thought Jessica. Yes, that was pretty much how it had been.

"And you can try and pretend that everything's okay." Roland was still talking. "You can act as if you think it matters whether you've done any schoolwork or what you eat or what you wear, but in the end . . . the pretending is such an effort, and you get so tired, that all you really want is for it to stop. For everything to stop."

His words jolted another memory in Jessica. It was the exact moment, walking back from school one Friday, when it had first occurred to her that there was a way to make it stop. A very simple way to finish with all the pain and the pretending and The Pit. And once the idea was in her mind, it had held a strange fascination. She had tried to push it away, but that only seemed to make it stronger. It was such a warm and comforting idea, such a reassurance when she was feeling so bad . . .

"And then once you've had the idea," said Roland, "it won't go away. You find yourself coming back to it again and again."

Jessica looked at him. "Did your friend tell you all this?"

Roland shook his head. "I didn't need anyone to tell me stuff like that," he said.

It was a moment before Jessica understood what he meant.

"You?" She stared at him. "Seriously?"

Roland gave a little snort. "Have you any idea how it feels to be like this?" He gestured down to the bulging mass of his body. "To have everyone looking at you wherever you go, staring, laughing, calling you names when they think you can't hear, calling you names when they know you can . . ." There was a bitterness in his voice as he continued. "You look around, and everyone else seems to be able to get up in the morning and smile and laugh and enjoy themselves . . . and you think, why can't I do that? Why can't I be *ordinary*? Why do I have to be different from everyone else?"

"And that's what gets to you in the end, isn't it?" It was Francis who was speaking now. "The being different. You want so much to be like everyone else but . . ." He looked sympathetically across at Roland as he spoke. "You know it's never going to happen. You're *always* going to be different. With you it's your weight; with me it was all *this*." He gestured to the drawings on the walls and the dolls on the shelves, then turned to Jessica with an odd, lopsided smile. "You remember that first day when you came and sat on the bench? That's what I'd gone there to think about. I don't know if I'd have actually done anything, but . . . that's what I was thinking about."

"So . . ." said Roland, "that means all three of us were . . ."

"Four."

The voice was Andi's, and she spoke with her gaze fixed firmly on the floor in front of her, her fingers picking aggressively at tufts in the carpet. "If you're talking about what it's like to be different, try being short and ugly when everyone else is tall and pretty. Try beating the living daylights out of anyone who dares to laugh at you . . . and then realizing that means there's no one left to talk to."

She looked up and stared defiantly at the faces around her. "I was all set to do it before Mum brought me over to meet Francis that day. And I'd have done it, too. I know I would, because things had gotten so bad that . . ." Her gaze returned to the carpet. "That it felt like the only way out."

For almost a minute, nobody spoke, and it was Francis who finally broke the silence.

"You know you thought we were all here to help Jessica?" he said, looking across at Roland. "Seems to me it's more like she's here to help us."

19

Neither Francis, nor Andi, nor Roland had ever told anyone they had been thinking about "ending it all," and to find they could share these thoughts and talk about them with others who had felt the same way was curiously liberating. It might sound strange, but they spent the rest of that morning talking—and sometimes even laughing—about how the idea had first occurred to them, how they had thought they might do it, and wondering whether any of them would really have gone through with it.

They looked at the newspaper articles that Roland had downloaded about Jessica's death—though there wasn't much to laugh at in them. The first was a description of how Jessica's body had been found by a woman walking her dog, and taken to the hospital, and the other was a description of the funeral, which, to Jessica's surprise, had been attended by several hundred people from the village and from her school. Reading about it was, she found, slightly embarrassing.

Jessica had never really considered that killing herself might have an effect on the lives of the people around her. She had thought, if she had thought about it at all, that her absence would probably make things easier for the people she knew. Nothing could have been further from the truth, as a look at the website her aunt had set up made clear.

On the site's home page was a big picture of Jessica—the same as the one that hung in the hall of the house on Bannock Lane—with a piece beneath it by Aunt Jo explaining how, after what had happened to her niece, she had given up her job and now spent her time trying to prevent something similar from happening to anyone else. She had trained as a counselor, set up the website, and if you wanted to get in touch with her, you could email her or call the number that was given at the top.

There were some interesting pages on the site describing the feelings that Jessica had privately called Being In The Pit—the feeling that nothing meant anything or ever could, of being different, of being completely alone.

There were a lot more pages on what caused people to feel this way and what they might do about it, with pieces by doctors on the medical causes and the drugs that can sometimes help you feel better, with descriptions by psychologists of techniques that some people had found helpful, phone numbers you could call, books you could read, websites you could visit, and—perhaps most interesting of all—pages of letters from people describing what it had been like for them, and what they had done to get themselves out of The Pit. Or to stop themselves falling back into it.

It was one of these letters that described something Jessica remembered and that the others instantly recognized as well. It talked about the extraordinary speed with which the feeling that life had no meaning could disappear on certain occasions and everything become normal again—for a while, at least. How one day you could be in the depths of despair and the next you could wake up feeling . . . okay. How little things like something someone said, or a scene from a film, or even a piece of music could change your mood in the blink of an eye. And how, when you were in one mood, the other seemed so silly. When the sun was out you could hardly remember the clouds and, when you were in The Pit, it was difficult to believe that sunshine had ever existed.

"Like me, yesterday morning," said Roland. "I was feeling really bad before you two came around." He nodded at Francis and Jessica. "But then, when I started talking to you, suddenly everything was different. I don't know why . . . It just was."

"I think it's the shock of seeing Jessica as a ghost that does that," said Andi. "It sort of snaps you out of yourself. I remember when Francis took me up to his room and Jessica walked through the middle of the bed . . . It was just so *interesting*. Much more interesting than being angry or miserable."

Francis did not think it was the shock of Jessica being a ghost that had caused his own mood to change. He thought Jessica had done that simply by . . . being Jessica. He had never really been interested in the fact that she was a ghost. It was Jessica as a friend that had made the difference.

Whatever the reason, however, the one thing they all agreed was that everything *had* changed since Jessica appeared. None of them had been in The Pit since they had met her. Which made Francis's idea—that the reason they could all see Jessica was so that she could stop them doing what she had done—particularly convincing.

Jessica herself was less sure.

"If it's true," she said, "that I'm here to stop you all making the same mistake I did, and I've done it . . . why am I *still* here?"

Everyone looked at Roland. He was the one who'd read the books and seemed to have all the answers.

"I suppose," he said, "the obvious answer is that there's someone else."

"Someone else?" Jessica frowned.

"Well, you were a ghost for almost a year before you met Francis," said Roland. "Then it was a few weeks before you met Andi. Then me yesterday. Why should it stop at three? Maybe there's someone else you still have to help."

They were still discussing this possibility when Francis glanced at his watch, saw it was lunchtime, and said that if anyone was hungry there was probably some bread and cheese in the kitchen.

"Oh, yes . . ." Roland gave a little cough. "I meant to say. Mum said I was to invite you all back for lunch at my house. If you want." He blushed slightly. "But it's all right. You don't have to come if . . ."

"Francis told me about the food your mum cooks," interrupted Andi. "And you have a pool as well, don't you? Can we go for a swim after?"

"Sure."

"Well, that settles it." Andi stood up. "Come on, you lot! Let's go!"

Francis watched as she and Roland headed for the stairs.

So that's it, he thought. You spend the morning talking about suicide with two other people who have been thinking about it and the ghost of someone who's already done it . . . and then you push off for lunch and a swim.

He glanced across at Jessica, who was thinking herself into a coat.

"Funny sort of morning," he said.

"Yes."

"Are you okay?"

"I think so." Jessica floated over to join him. "That first day, when I came and sat beside you on the bench . . . You said you were wondering about it then."

"Yes."

"You never said anything."

"No."

"Not to anyone?"

"No."

"Nor did I," said Jessica. "And looking back on it, that was definitely a mistake."

20

Lunch at Roland's house was a remarkably cheerful affair. Mrs. Boyle had roasted three chickens, along with a mountain of roast potatoes, roast vegetables, sausages, bacon, bread sauce, onion gravy, and a basket of freshly baked rolls in case anyone had the odd corner that still needed filling.

Roland's father carved the chickens. He was a tough, wiry-looking man not much bigger than his wife, and Francis couldn't help wondering how two such diminutive people could have produced a son who was bigger than both of them put together.

When Jessica got Andi to ask Mr. Boyle what he did for a living, they discovered he had started out as a crane operator before borrowing enough money to buy his own crane and, finally, setting up his own company.

"He goes all over the country," said Mrs. Boyle proudly. "You want something heavy lifted, my Ronnie's the man to do it!"

He had, it turned out, recently been involved in lifting railway carriages from a steep embankment after a passenger train had come off the line near Doncaster. And while Mrs. Boyle cleared the plates before bringing out the desserts—two apple pies, a large bowl of chocolate mousse, a fruit salad, and a jug of cream—Mr. Boyle used some spare silverware and some string to give a demonstration of the problems involved in lifting something weighing fifty tons without it slipping out of the harness and killing the people underneath.

When lunch was over, Francis and Andi offered to help with the dishes, but Mrs. Boyle wouldn't hear of it.

"Ronnie and I will look after all that," she said, shooing them toward the door. "You go and watch one of Rollo's films or play on his computer. Save your energy for a swim later."

Roland had an impressive collection of films and games, but Andi took one look at his room—with the soda cans littering the floor, the plates with the half-eaten remains of food, and the dirt and dust—and said there was no way she was doing anything until there was somewhere she could sit down without risking serious infection.

Before they knew it, Roland had been dispatched to find a vacuum, dusters, and cleaning fluid, Jessica had been told to float up in one corner of the room and keep out of the way, and Francis had been sent back to the kitchen with a pile of dirty plates, and told to bring back some garbage bags.

Mrs. Boyle asked what he wanted the garbage bags for.

"Roland's tidying his room a bit," Francis explained, "and he needs something to put the trash in."

"Tidying his room?" Mrs. Boyle stared at him. "Really?"

"It was Andi's idea," Francis admitted. "She sort of told him he had to."

"And he's *doing* it?" Mr. Boyle looked equally astonished.

"Andi can be quite forceful when she sets her mind to something," said Francis. "I don't think she gave him much choice."

Mrs. Boyle had taken a roll of black garbage bags from a drawer but did not pass them to Francis. "If you don't mind, I'll take these in myself." She headed toward the door. "Perhaps she can get him to change his sheets at the same time . . ."

"I'll look after those, shall I?" Mr. Boyle gestured to the pile of plates Francis was carrying. He took the plates, scraped the bits of food into a trash can, and began loading them into the dishwasher. "She hasn't been able to get into his room for weeks, you know. Roland wouldn't let her. He wouldn't let *anyone* in. I don't mind telling you, we were getting worried. We knew he was unhappy about something . . . but we didn't know what, and he wouldn't say. He wouldn't see anyone, didn't want to go out . . ." Mr. Boyle turned to look across at Francis. "And then you come along and . . . bingo . . . all the lights are back on and he's asking if he can invite people for lunch! I don't know what you did to him, but . . . What *did* you do to him?"

"Nothing, really," said Francis. "We just . . . talked, you know."

"Talked . . ." Mr. Boyle let out a long sigh. "We tried that. Trouble was, we could never get him to talk back. But Angela says you had him chatting away almost as soon as you walked in the door. She doesn't know how you did it, but . . ." He paused, a frown of concern on his face as he looked carefully at Francis. "Are you all right? You look a bit tired."

It was only now it was mentioned that Francis realized he *was* tired. Very tired. It had, looking back on it, been an eventful morning.

"Why don't you go and lie down?" said Mr. Boyle. "Leave the tidying up to the others, and go and have a rest. Use one of the loungers by the pool."

"Yes," said Francis. "I think I will."

He walked through to the pool, lay down on one of the loungers, and fell almost instantly asleep.

● ● ●

When he woke, it was to find Jessica lying on the lounger beside him, propped up on one elbow, looking at him.

"You've been drooling," she said.

"Thank you." Francis pushed himself up to a sitting position and noticed that someone had covered him with a blanket.

"That was Roland's mum," Jessica told him. "She's been coming in every quarter of an hour to check you're all right."

"Oh . . ."

"She comes on tiptoe, so as not to wake you. The others wanted to come in earlier for a swim, but she wouldn't let them. She said you needed your rest."

"Ah . . ."

"She and Mr. Boyle have been talking about you in the kitchen. They think you have magic powers. Seriously. They think you do miracles. At the moment they're discussing how long it might take you to get Roland back to school."

"Ah." Francis still had no idea what, if anything, he was going to do about that one.

"Don't worry!" Jessica smiled. "We'll think of something. But in the meantime, I'd better tell Andi and Roland they can come in for a swim!"

And she disappeared.

• • •

Later—much later—after a swim, a very large dinner, another swim, and a movie Roland provided about a man chained by his leg to a radiator, who had to choose between starving to death and cutting off his own foot to get free, Roland's parents took Francis to one side, as he was getting ready to leave, and asked if he had had a chance yet to talk to Roland about school.

"No . . ." said Francis. "Not yet."

"Frieda Campion told me you like to wait for the right time," said Mrs. Boyle. "She said that, with her daughter, you waited till she was feeling secure before you . . . did whatever it is you do."

"Well, it wasn't quite like that . . ."

"Unfortunately," Mr. Boyle interrupted, "we don't have a lot of time. You see, Roland's been out of school a month, and they're making a fuss about it already. Threatening social services, legal action, all that sort of thing."

"So if you could have a word with him, fairly quickly," Mrs. Boyle put in.

"I will talk to him," said Francis, "but, honestly . . . I'm not sure it will do any good. I can't make him do something he doesn't want to do, can I?"

Mr. Boyle readily agreed that this would indeed be impossible, and Mrs. Boyle said they were just grateful to him for trying, but he could see in their eyes that neither of them believed him.

Roland's parents were both quite convinced that Francis was going to produce another miracle.

21

In the week that followed, Roland biked over to Alma Road each day to spend the evening with his new friends—in fact, he was usually waiting for them outside in the street when they got home from school—and he would stay until Francis's or Andi's mother told him it was time to go home.

They were sitting in the attic at number forty-seven—Jessica was helping Andi finish off some math homework—when Francis cautiously asked Roland if he'd thought at all about when he might go back to school. You could almost see the shutters close down behind Roland's eyes as soon as the idea was mentioned.

"I'm not going back," he said, his chin jutting out determinedly. "Not ever. I don't care what anyone says. I'm not going back."

"But . . . don't you have to?" asked Francis. "I mean, everyone has to go to school, don't they? It's the law."

"I don't care," Roland repeated stubbornly. "I'm not going. And no one can make me. I'd rather die."

In the circumstances, this was not a threat to be taken lightly, and Francis let the matter drop. He had said he would talk to Roland about school and he had done so. It hadn't worked—he had never really expected that it would—but he had fulfilled his promise and, much as he would like to have helped, he didn't see what else he could do.

It was later the same evening, after Roland had walked Andi back to number thirty-nine before cycling home himself, that Jessica came up with a possible solution to the problem.

"I wonder," she said, "if anyone's thought about homeschooling?"

Francis looked up from the broken zipper he was removing from Andi's school skirt before putting in a new one. "Home what?"

"Homeschooling," Jessica repeated. "The law says you have to learn somewhere, but if your parents want to teach you at home, they can."

"Really?" This was news to Francis.

"I had a friend who did it for years," said Jessica. "I don't suppose Roland's dad would have time to do much, but his mum might."

Francis considered the idea. "Interesting. I wonder if Roland will go for it."

When they told him about it the next evening, Roland went for the idea immediately. The thought that there might be some way of never going to school again, and it somehow being all right, seemed almost too good to be true. An hour on his laptop, trawling through various websites, quickly convinced him that it was indeed perfectly possible. If homeschooling was what you wanted to try, there were dozens of places you could go to for help setting it up and, according to the people who'd done it, it wasn't that difficult. Mostly what it took was a lot of time.

"Dad's too busy, so it'd have to be Mum doing most of it," he said, closing the lid of the laptop. "But I'm not sure she'll want to. She gets very nervous about anything connected with schoolwork. She had a panic attack helping me with my homework when I was seven." He paused. "But I could ask."

"How about getting Francis to ask?" said Jessica. "I don't know if you've noticed, but your parents think

149

Francis could walk on water if he put his mind to it. If he said homeschooling was the thing to do, I don't think there'd be much argument from either of them."

• • •

Francis put the idea to Mr. and Mrs. Boyle on Saturday. He sat down with them at the kitchen table before lunch, while Roland had taken Andi off for a swim, and he began by telling them that, after speaking to Roland, he did not think it would be a good idea to try and get him to return to St. Saviour's.

"Oh, dear." Mrs. Boyle could not disguise her disappointment. "Are you sure?"

"I think if he went back now," said Francis, "it would just make him very unhappy. And that wouldn't be good, would it?"

"Maybe not," said Mr. Boyle, "but he *has* to go back, doesn't he? It's the law."

"Not necessarily," said Francis. He explained, with Jessica prompting him, how homeschooling was the legal right of every parent, that he knew of someone who had done it and found it a lot less difficult than they expected, and that there were all sorts of places to go for help, if Mrs. Boyle was prepared to take it on.

"Me?" Mrs. Boyle's eyes widened. "I couldn't teach him! I don't know anything!"

"Like I said, there's all these organizations that'll help you set it up," Francis assured her. "Roland's been finding out about them on the Internet. They tell you what to do, what books to get and everything. My friend said it takes a lot of time, but it's really not as difficult as you might think."

"And you reckon this learning at home would be the best thing for Rollo, do you?" asked Mr. Boyle.

"Yes," said Francis. "Yes, I do."

Mr. Boyle looked across at his wife. "Well, it's up to you, love. You're the one who'd have to do most of the work. But if Francis says it's the best thing . . ."

And, as Jessica had said, that was the clinching argument, really. Francis was, after all, the young man who, in a few brief days, had turned their son's life around. If he said homeschooling was the answer, then that was what they would try, however frightening the prospect might be for Mrs. Boyle.

• • •

The lessons, once they began, went better than either Roland or his mother had expected. As a home tutor,

Mrs. Boyle might have the disadvantage of knowing almost nothing about any of the subjects her son needed to study but, where Roland's happiness was concerned, she could be very determined. By the end of the week, she had a large chart on the kitchen wall showing lesson plans for the month ahead, she had a list by the phone of people she could contact for help, and the kitchen table was covered in books on the causes of the First World War, Spanish vocabulary, and the ecology of the Amazon basin.

During the lessons, Roland usually found himself explaining things to his mother rather than the other way around, but he was not the first person to discover that this is in fact one of the best ways to learn. If they were both stuck, there was no shortage of people they could call, though Roland preferred to start by asking Jessica. She usually came by two or three times during the day to see how things were going and, if she did not know the answer herself, she could always get Francis or Andi to ask a teacher at John Felton. Among the four of them, there weren't many problems that couldn't be sorted out.

When Roland finished his work in the afternoon, he would get on his bike and hurry over to Alma Road.

Regular cycling meant he was much better at coping with the journey these days, and he barely needed to stop and catch his breath before pushing open the front door and climbing the stairs to the attic room in Francis's house, or at Andi's.

At the weekends, the four usually met at Roland's. His home, after all, had the swimming pool, not to mention the attraction of Mrs. Boyle's cooking. They would swim, lie around, talk, eat—and if you had been watching them splashing noisily in the pool, you would have found it hard to believe that, only a few short weeks before, three of them had been seriously considering how best to end their own lives, and one of them already had.

They looked like people who were enjoying life—as indeed they were—though there was one incident, three weeks after the great revelation about Jessica, that threatened to blow their new lives apart.

22

It was a Wednesday, and Francis had had a message from his teacher that Mrs. Parsons wanted to see him at recess. He was not unduly worried. On previous occasions when he had spoken to the principal she had been quite friendly—but when he arrived at her office this time, there was no smile on her face as she gestured him to sit down.

"I've had a complaint," she said, looking directly at him across her desk, "from Quentin Howard. He says Andi Campion attacked him outside the gym five weeks ago, and it's left him almost too frightened to come in to school. He says you were there when it happened. Is that true?"

Francis wasn't sure how to answer this. If Jessica had been there, he would have been able to ask her advice, but Jessica had gone to London with a class of textiles students to see a Vivienne Westwood exhibition at the Victoria and Albert Museum.

He could have lied, but Francis decided against it. He had never been good at lying and he had a feeling Mrs. Parsons was probably going to get to the truth one way or another.

"Yes, I was there," he said. "But it wasn't really like Quentin said."

"No?" The principal leaned back in her chair. "So tell me how it was."

And Francis found himself telling her what had happened—what Quentin had said, how Andi had hit him, twice, and then about all the times Quentin had teased him in the past and how much of a difference it had made to his life now that the teasing had stopped.

Mrs. Parsons listened to it all in silence.

"I see," she said, when he had finished. "I think maybe we should hear what Quentin has to say about all this." She pressed a button on the intercom on her desk and asked the secretary to send him in.

He was looking thinner, Francis noticed. There were dark rings under his eyes, he was clearly nervous, and he had a twitch on one side of his face—but what he said was interesting. Quentin insisted, when Mrs.

Parsons asked, that all his remarks about dolls and knitting had only ever been meant as a joke. He had no idea, he said, that they might have been upsetting Francis. They were just a bit of fun, and he said all this so earnestly and with such an air of desperation that Francis was inclined to believe him.

Nor had Francis realized how badly Quentin had been affected by Andi hitting him. It had left him very frightened. So frightened, it emerged, that he had been making up excuses not to come to school—which was why the whole matter had come to Mrs. Parsons's attention.

Francis almost felt sorry for him but, at the time, he was more concerned about what might happen to Andi. Mrs. Parsons had said on Andi's first day that if she was involved in any sort of fight she would have to leave, and the principal was not the sort of person to make idle threats.

It was a close-run thing. When Andi was finally hauled into the office, there were, Mrs. Parsons told her, only two reasons why she was not already on her way home. One was that she had had an excellent series of reports from her teachers—who all seemed to think that she was settling in well and making good use of her time at school—but more important than that, said Mrs. Parsons, was an appeal on her behalf from Quentin.

"Quentin asked for you not to be thrown out?" Francis had been waiting for Andi outside the office to hear what had happened, and was understandably puzzled. "Why would he do that?"

Andi gave a shrug. "He said he realized it was partly his fault, and it didn't seem fair for me to get all the blame. He said as long as I promised not to hit him again, he was okay."

"So you didn't get punished at all?" asked Francis.

"Three weeks litter duty," said Andi, as they set off down the corridor. "I can live with that." She took his arm. "If I *had* been thrown out, would you have missed me?"

"Hugely," said Francis. "In fact, I'd probably have had to kill myself."

And for some reason that made both of them laugh.

● ● ●

Jessica thought Andi had had a lucky escape.

"If Quentin hadn't stepped in, Mrs. Parsons would have thrown her out. I know she would," she said. "I wonder why he did?"

"I wonder why I didn't tell him to stop with the teasing, like you suggested," said Francis. "I don't know if he *would* have stopped, but I should have tried."

As Andi was still doing her litter duty and Roland had had to go to the dentist, it was just the two of them sitting on the sofa in the attic of number forty-seven. After hearing the story of what had happened with Mrs. Parsons that day, the conversation turned to Jessica's trip to London.

The day out at the Victoria and Albert Museum had had its ups and downs—Jackie Wilmot had thrown up on Miss Jossaume on the bus, and there was a story that someone had seen Lorna Gilchrist stealing books from the museum shop—but the exhibition itself had more than made up for all of that.

Vivienne Westwood was a designer they both admired enormously, and as a ghost, Jessica was able not only to describe the costumes she had seen but to show them. Francis sat on the sofa while she modeled one outfit after another, finishing up with a dress made from an Aztec print with an angular hem that Francis particularly admired and said suited her brilliantly. The next time the school organized a trip to the V&A,

he said, he would have to insist on being allowed to go with them.

One way and another it had been a good day for both of them, though Jessica found she was left with the odd feeling that she had *missed* something.

"It's a bit like when I was at the hospital," she said, trying to explain what she meant, "on the day I found I was dead, you know? When I felt there was something I should be doing."

"I seem to remember the trouble then was you had no idea *what* you were supposed to be doing," said Francis.

"I didn't. I still don't. But I've been thinking about what Roland said—about there being someone else, and how I need to find them so I can move on. I wondered if maybe I shouldn't go out and start looking for them."

"I don't see how you can," said Francis. "Unless you plan on walking around town and shouting to ask if anyone can hear you."

This was in fact pretty much what Jessica had had in mind.

"It might work, mightn't it?"

"It might," said Francis, "but I doubt it."

"Why?"

"Well, if I was walking around town and heard someone shouting, 'Can anyone hear me? I'm a ghost and I need to talk to you,' I'd probably start walking in the other direction as fast as possible."

"Ah . . ." Jessica sighed. "I hadn't thought of that."

"And anyway, it's not how it's worked before, is it?" Francis continued. "I mean, you didn't have to look for me, did you? You didn't have to look for any of us. We were just . . . there."

"So I should just sit around and wait?"

"That wouldn't be so bad, would it?" said Francis. "I don't know about you, but I'm quite enjoying all this. I've got three friends now—one of whom has a swimming pool, another who makes me feel like I'm protected by a trained bodyguard, and a third who is not only incredibly beautiful but goes around after school in a Vivienne Westwood original . . . I'm having the best time I've had in years."

From downstairs, there came the sound of the front doorbell.

"That'll be Andi. I'd better let her in." Francis headed for the stairs, but turned before leaving. "I know Roland's friend said it was important that you move on and not be stuck here, but I don't want you to go. I don't want you to go anywhere. As far as I'm concerned, the longer you stay the better."

Jessica watched him leave, and decided that perhaps he was right. Maybe there was no real need for her to *do* anything. If there was someone else who needed her help, they would turn up—or not—in their own good time. In the meantime, she could, as Francis said, make the most of things while she waited. Enjoy her friends. Enjoy their company. Enjoy being together . . .

And what was that other thing Francis had said? *Incredibly beautiful . . .*

Jessica smiled to herself.

Funny if he was right about that as well . . .

23

At Easter, Roland's mother took all four of them on vacation to Center Parcs at Longleat Forest. Mrs. Boyle thought she was only taking three people, of course, but none of them would have gone without Jessica, who took up very little room in the car, sitting in the middle of the backseat.

Center Parcs is chiefly designed for families that enjoy outdoor leisure activities and, despite the fact that Francis had no great interest in sports and that Jessica was a ghost, it worked remarkably well. The apartment they had rented was spacious and comfortable and almost the first thing Francis discovered when they arrived was about a hundred back issues of *Harper's Bazaar* left in one of the cupboards. He and Jessica spent a large part of the vacation sitting by the pool flipping through the pages and taking notes, and occasionally joining Andi and Roland as they swam, roamed the woods on bicycles, played badminton, rode horses, and climbed rocks.

Andi thought days spent doing things out of doors were sheer heaven, and Roland was usually the one who kept her company. Why someone so bulky should be prepared to climb rocks or bike for miles when he was clearly designed to spend most of his day sitting in front of a computer was a mystery, but that was what he did. When Andi suggested another swim, Roland would stand up and get his towel. If she suggested a bike ride or a bit of rock climbing, he was out there, strapping on his safety gear. If she wanted to climb a tree, play a few sets of tennis, or do a circuit of the assault course, Roland was right behind her. He might look as if the effort was killing him, but he was always there.

It puzzled Francis. "Why does he do it?" he asked Jessica one day as they watched Roland and Andi battling it out on the badminton court. "I mean, he can't enjoy it, can he?"

"It's because he likes her." Jessica was standing behind him, massaging his shoulders.

"I know he likes her," said Francis, relaxing in the warmth that spread through the muscles of his back. "We all do, but—"

"No," Jessica interrupted. "I don't mean that way. I mean . . . he *likes* her."

Francis was quite taken aback. Andi? Roland *liked* Andi? He stared at the two of them out on the court.

Roland, despite his size, was able to give his opponent a good run for her money in a badminton game. He was big, but he was surprisingly nimble and had a knack of flicking the shuttle to just the point where it would drop out of Andi's reach. As Francis watched, he won the game and Andi threw down her racket in disgust, ran over to Roland, pushed him to the ground, and started pummeling his chest. She was hitting him quite hard but Roland didn't seem to mind. For all his protests, it looked as if he was having a thoroughly good time.

"Does she know? That he likes her?"

"Oh, yes!" Jessica smiled.

"And she doesn't mind?"

"I think . . ." Jessica put her head to one side. "That someone liking her like that is something she's never had before, and she's rather enjoying it."

It explained a lot, thought Francis. It explained why Roland always did whatever Andi suggested. Why he followed her around like some huge devoted spaniel. Why he was always asking what she wanted to do. Thinking about it, it also explained why he turned down so many cookies and snacks these days, like he was on some sort of diet.

Once it was pointed out, Francis wondered why he hadn't seen it before. Roland did indeed like Andi. He would have walked through fire for her, and in a way that was what she asked him to do.

Because it was Andi who told Roland he should go back to school.

● ● ●

"Why would I want to go back to school?" Roland was plainly puzzled when it was first suggested. "I hated it there."

"I'm not saying you should go back to St. Saviour's," said Andi. "I'm saying you should come to school with us. At John Felton. Then we can all be together during the day, not just in the evenings." She threaded an arm through his. "You could join the badminton club. We could help each other in class. I think we'd have a really good time."

The words "good time" and "school" did not fit in the same space in Roland's head, but this was Andi asking him. The thought of being with her all day through the spring term was the strongest possible temptation. Even so, he wasn't sure.

He was still uncertain on the last Saturday of vacation, when the four of them were out shopping. They were in Dummer's department store, and Andi was in the changing room with Jessica, trying on clothes, while the two boys waited outside.

"The thing is," Roland was saying, "I can't see it would be any different at your school than it was at mine. I'm still the same shape. People would still be laughing at me and saying things behind my back . . ."

"I don't think so," said Francis.

"Why not?"

"Two reasons." Francis ticked them off on his fingers. "One is that we've got this new principal who makes a real fuss if people do things like that. And the second is that everyone'll know if they said anything rude to you, Andi would beat them to a pulp. She can be quite scary, you know."

"I'm not sure I want Andi to beat up anyone for me." Roland sat gloomily on a bench, his chin in his hands. "It's nice to know she would if I asked, but . . ."

"You wouldn't have to ask," said Francis. "I've never asked her to lay a finger on anyone. But I promise you, as soon as people know you're a friend of hers, no one will dare say anything. That's all it takes."

Roland looked doubtful, but at that moment the curtain of the changing room swept back and Andi appeared. She was wearing a tiny micro skirt and an even tinier sparkly boob tube. Jessica was wearing the same.

"Ta-da!" The two of them flung out their arms, took up a pose, and grinned at the two boys.

"What do you think?" asked Andi.

"I thought you were supposed to be trying on the pants," said Francis.

Roland said nothing. He simply stared, but inside, that was the moment he made his decision. He would go back to school. Whatever happened, if it meant he could spend more time with Andi, it would be worth it.

● ● ●

Francis was given the job of explaining things to Roland's mother. He was a little concerned that, after all the time and money she had invested in home-schooling, Mrs. Boyle might not be overjoyed at the news that her son had decided, after all, to go back to school.

He could not have been more wrong. Her instant reaction to the news was a great cry of delight and a long, rather embarrassing hug. Her Roland was going back to school! She could scarcely believe it! He would go off in the morning with his friends like a normal boy and come home, happy, at the end of it. It was how she had always dreamed it should be.

How Francis had done it, she had no idea, but she suspected he had planned the whole thing this way from the start. He had deliberately let Roland relax for a couple of months, let him regain his confidence by some time at home, and now he was bringing him back into school. The skill with which he had managed it all left her awestruck.

"You're sure he's ready for it, are you?" she asked as they sat at the kitchen table. "You don't think anything will . . . happen?"

"I don't think so," said Francis, "But if it does, he's got Andi and me to help sort it out."

"Of course he has." Mrs. Boyle reached across the table and patted his hand. "And Ronnie and I are so grateful to you. I'll ring your Mrs. Parsons tomorrow and arrange an interview."

"Great." Francis stood up. "I'll go and tell Roland."

"I was going to ask your advice about one other thing," said Mrs. Boyle, "if you had the time?"

"Yes, of course." Francis sat down again.

"Doing all this with Rollo . . ." Mrs. Boyle gestured to the textbooks that littered the table. "I found the work wasn't quite as difficult as I'd expected, and it occurred to me I might carry on, and maybe even take one or two GCSE exams." Absentmindedly, she took a strip of paper and began twisting it around her fingers. "Do you think that sounds silly?"

Francis wasn't sure what to say.

"You want to take some exams?"

"I know I'm probably too old, and I'm not as clever as all of you . . ."

"She's brighter than most of the people at John Felton," said Jessica, "and she works really hard. Tell her to go for it."

"I think you're smarter than most of the people I know at school," said Francis, "and you work really hard. I think you should go for it."

Mrs. Boyle blushed; then a great smile spread across her face. "Thank you," she said. "I was hoping you'd say that."

24

Roland's mother went to see Mrs. Parsons the next Monday, and she agreed that Roland could join the school. There was a slight delay while they waited for his uniform to arrive but, by the third week of the spring term, he was ready to go and, once he started, it was all easier than he could have imagined.

Francis was right. Nobody commented on his size. When he came into a classroom, nobody said anything. Most people didn't even look at him. They glanced up when he arrived and then got on with their work or whatever they were doing. The teachers seemed to know who he was and to be expecting him, so there were no long embarrassing introductions to make. They told him where to go, let him sit down, and got on with the class.

Roland even enjoyed the lessons. Being with his friends was a lot more fun than sitting at home in the kitchen with his mother. It was good to sit beside Andi and Francis, watching Jessica float up and down through the floor, and it was very good to stroll out with them at recess and sit on the bench on the far side of the playing field in the sun.

Mrs. Parsons had arranged for Roland to be in the same class as Andi and Francis for most of his classes, but in one subject this had not been possible. Roland did Spanish as his foreign language—his parents had a house in Andorra—while Francis and Andi did French, and it was this that led to an unfortunate incident on his first day.

The class itself was no problem. Jessica had gone with Roland to make sure he knew where to go and to keep him company, and the work was, if anything, a little easier than he remembered from St. Saviour's. But at lunchtime, as Jessica was showing him the way back to the bench where they had all arranged to meet for lunch, someone shouted at Roland to wait.

Roland stopped and turned around, as a boy came over and stared at him.

"You are enormous," he said. "I mean, we've got some fat people here, but you are . . . huge!"

"Walk away," said Jessica. "Come on, walk away!"

But Roland did not walk away. He stood there staring at the ground as the boy reached out and lifted his jacket.

"Look at that!" said the boy. "You've got rolls of you pouring over the top of your pants!"

Jessica opened her mouth to say something, then changed her mind and disappeared. An instant later, she was standing by Francis on the bench by the playing field.

"Where's Andi?" she asked.

"Gone to the bathroom, I think." Francis looked up. "Why?"

"It's Roland. Dermot's poking fun at him. Over there."

She pointed across the field, to where Dermot was quite literally poking Roland quizzically in the stomach.

"It feels a bit like a water balloon, doesn't it?" he was saying. "I mean, you can actually lift it right up and then . . ."

"Stop that!" Francis was racing across the field toward him, shouting at the top of his voice. "Leave him alone!"

Dermot looked around in surprise.

"What do you think you're doing?" Francis was panting as he ran up to stand by Roland. "Leave him alone!"

"I'm not *doing* anything!" Dermot let go of Roland's blazer. "I'm just looking."

"You're making fun of him," said Francis, "and you've no right!"

"Why don't you mind your own business!" said Dermot. "It's nothing to do with you."

"It *is* to do with me," said Francis angrily. "He's my friend and even if he wasn't my friend it'd still be my business."

At that moment Mr. Anderson, one of the PE teachers, appeared.

"What's going on?" he asked.

"Dermot was laughing at Roland for being fat," said Francis.

"No, I wasn't!" said Dermot. "I wasn't laughing. I never laughed."

"He told Roland he was enormous," said Jessica, "and he said we've got some fat people here, but you're huge."

"He told Roland he was enormous," said Francis. "And he said 'we've got some fat people here, but you're huge.'"

"Oh, for goodness' sake!" Mr. Anderson gave Dermot a look of exasperation. "Don't you ever listen? Didn't you *hear* what Mrs. Parsons said in assembly?"

"What assembly?" said Dermot. "I've been away."

"Right . . ." Mr. Anderson took a deep breath. "Go and stand over there and wait." He turned back to Roland. "I'm sorry you had to put up with that on your first day. Are you all right?"

"Yes," said Roland. "Yes, I think so."

"I shall go and explain some of the rules of good manners to Master Dermot," said Mr. Anderson, "and I promise he will not trouble you again. Now, if you want to make a formal complaint . . ."

"No, no," said Roland. "It's all right."

"Okay . . ." Mr. Anderson nodded. "Well, if you change your mind, let me know." And he walked across to Dermot.

Andi was waiting for them by the bench on the playing field.

"Jessica's told me what happened," she said. "Don't worry, I'll be having a word with that little worm and . . ."

"No," said Roland. "Please don't. You'll only get into trouble!"

"I don't care about that," said Andi. "He's not getting away with it . . ."

"No, please! Really!" Roland insisted. "I'd rather you didn't do anything. It didn't matter. It really . . . didn't matter."

And it was only when he said the words that he realized they were true. *It didn't matter!* Someone had come up and told him he was fat and . . . it just wasn't important. A few months before, an incident like that would have left him crying in the bathroom until it was time to go home, but now . . . now all he could think about was why on earth he hadn't told Dermot to leave, or simply walked away.

The thing he had most feared would happen *had* happened, but for some reason it had been okay. Perhaps it was because there were people around him who said it was not okay; perhaps that was what made the difference. Or maybe it was simply the realization that someone telling him he was fat wasn't that important. It didn't mean anything. And if the same thing happened tomorrow, it wouldn't mean anything then, either.

"You're sure you're okay?" asked Francis.

"I'm fine," said Roland.

He took a deep breath and grinned.

"Really, I'm fine!"

25

After a day with her friends, Jessica would return, as she did every evening, to the room at the hospital where she had first discovered she was dead. The time she returned might vary a little from day to day, but it was usually somewhere between eight and nine o'clock. She still had no idea why she went back there, but the need to do so had the same sort of compulsion that makes some people keep washing their hands or avoid stepping on cracks in the sidewalk.

Francis was the first to notice that the time at which she went back seemed to be getting earlier. As the spring term progressed, he noted that she was usually gone before eight, and that sometimes it was closer to seven.

Jessica tried, when this was pointed out to her, to make herself stay a bit longer, but whatever the force was that drove her to return to the room on the third floor, it was quite impossible to resist. When she had to go, she had to go.

She asked Roland if he knew of any reason why all this might be happening, but he said he didn't. Nor, when he inquired, did his friend in Australia.

"She said you'll just have to hope it doesn't get any worse," he reported, "and that you don't find you're stuck at the hospital all day as well as all night!"

It was an alarming thought.

"I'm quite sure that's never going to happen," said Francis firmly. "We're only talking about an hour or so, aren't we? I'm sure it's nothing to worry about."

It might only be an hour or so, but Jessica *did* worry. Quite apart from the prospect of it getting worse, there were already occasions when it could be inconvenient. At the weekend, if they were watching a movie or Andi's mother was taking them out for a meal, she could suddenly find that everyone around her had disappeared and she was back at the hospital. It would happen without warning and was oddly disconcerting.

And of course it meant she missed out completely on things like Mrs. Boyle's trip to the theater.

● ● ●

Roland's mother had organized the theater trip to celebrate her son's successful return to school. She had bought tickets for a revival of *The Rocky Horror Show* down in Southampton. She had heard it had some wonderfully offbeat costumes that she thought Francis would enjoy, and he was indeed looking forward to it, but he was disappointed when, shortly before leaving, Jessica announced that she would not be coming.

"No?" Francis looked up from the seam of the shift dress he was tacking. "Why? Is something wrong?"

"Not really, no, it's just . . . I have to get back to the hospital," said Jessica. "Now."

"Oh." Francis had known that Jessica would not be able to see all the show, but she had been planning to see at least the first half. Glancing at the clock, he saw it was barely six o'clock. She had never had to leave this early before.

"Okay." He did his best to look unconcerned. "Well, I'll see you tomorrow. Tell you all about it then."

"Yes . . ." Jessica opened her mouth to say something else, but before she could speak, Francis's mother called up the stairs to say that the car had arrived and Mrs. Boyle and the others were waiting.

Francis went to the top of the stairs to tell her he was on his way, but by the time he turned back to hear whatever it was Jessica wanted to say . . .

. . . she had gone.

• • •

Several hours later at the hospital, Jessica wondered for the umpteenth time what could possibly be making her return there with such regularity and such insistence. It wasn't as if she did anything when she got there. Except stand and look out the window at the parking garage on the other side of the road. She didn't mind being there exactly—it was a little tedious, perhaps, but you got used to it—she just wondered what could possibly be the point.

And she wondered, too, what would happen if what Roland's friend in Australia suggested came true. What if the urge to return to the hospital *did* grow to the point where she needed to be there most of the day, as well as all of the night? How would she manage if she could no longer be with her friends? What would she do if . . .

A movement in the road beneath her interrupted her thoughts. There was someone she recognized walking up the hill. It was a girl from Francis's class at school—Lorna, Lorna Gilchrist—and Jessica wondered what she was doing.

It didn't look as if she had been in an accident, and it was too late to be attending one of the clinics, so she was probably visiting a relative or a friend, Jessica thought. Except that, at the top of the road, instead of entering the hospital, Lorna turned left and walked across the tarmac to the entrance to the parking garage.

It was an odd place to go on her own. It was past ten o'clock, the sun had set, and the parking garage at night was not a place that Jessica liked to walk through alone, even as a ghost. There was supposed to be a security guard at the entrance but he wasn't always there . . . and why *was* Lorna on her own?

Jessica found herself drifting out the window and through the air above the road. Maybe she was meeting someone. Maybe the person she was meeting had a car parked there and was waiting . . . But no, that couldn't be right, because now Lorna had emerged from the staircase on to the top floor of the parking garage, and there wasn't a car or a soul in sight.

The fact that she was alone did not seem to bother Lorna. She was carrying a small bag and she walked straight over to the parapet at the far side and looked out over the town. In the deepening twilight, the lights of the city spread out below her, sloping down to the floodlit cathedral with its huge central tower. In one quick move, Lorna pulled herself up on to the parapet, swung her legs over, and sat there, staring out at the view.

It made Jessica a little nervous. The parking garage was built on a hill and the drop on that side was six floors, straight down to an area of concrete pavement. If Lorna were to slip, or if she lost her balance for any reason, she could kill herself. But Lorna clearly wasn't worried. She took out a worn, stuffed dog from her bag, sat him on the parapet beside her, then leaned forward and peered down to ground below.

It was only then that Jessica realized what was happening.

She knew exactly why Lorna was here, and what she was planning to do.

She was going to jump.

Lorna was going to jump.

26

Jumping from the roof of the parking garage was something Lorna Gilchrist had been planning for some weeks, and both the time and the place had been carefully chosen. She had worked out the height required for someone of her weight to kill herself in the fall—she was a smart girl, and good with numbers—and she had calculated that, as long as she fell headfirst, the hundred and thirty feet to the ground were more than enough to break her neck.

She was not quite sure when she had made the final decision. It had crept up on her in the last few months, but there was no doubt in her mind that it was the right one. She could not carry on with things as they were, and there was no other way out that she could see. In the circumstances, jumping headfirst from the top story of a parking garage seemed not only reasonable, but absolutely the best thing to do.

Eight months before, Lorna's father had gone missing. Mr. Gilchrist was a lawyer, who went to work one morning and didn't come back. No one knew what had happened to him. Mrs. Gilchrist did not know if her husband had been run over by a car, kidnapped, or suffered a memory loss. Nor did anyone else until, after five months of uncertainty, a policeman arrived at the house to say Mr. Gilchrist had been found, and that he was working as a waiter in London, living with a woman he had met at a bus stop. Since the day he'd left, Lorna had not seen or heard a single word from him.

It was a shock, a terrible shock, but Lorna might have coped if, at the same time, things hadn't been so bad at school. She never knew why Denise Ritchie and Angela Wyman had decided to tell stories about her— she supposed that, for some reason, they didn't like her—but, whatever the reason, it was very painful.

It was Denise who spread the story that Lorna wet her pants at school and had to bring in clean underwear and change twice a day. She would say it as if she felt sorry for Lorna, but when in class she put a hand up and asked for the window to be opened because there was a smell, everyone knew what she meant, including Lorna.

Angela, not to be outdone, started the story that Lorna stole things from the local shops, though she always insisted, as she passed this on, that she was sure it wasn't true. Then, if something ever went missing from someone's bag at school, she would sigh and tut and make it clear that, sadly, she knew who was probably responsible.

There were literally dozens of such stories, each of them more cruel than the last, and although at first few people believed them, over time they gathered a certain strength. Then Denise came in one day with the story that Lorna's father had run away with a girl not much older than Lorna, who he'd met at a bus stop. And when it turned out that *was* true, people wondered if some of the other stuff might not be as well.

A doctor, if she had seen one, could have told Lorna that she was clinically depressed, and explained how this affected the chemistry of her brain. But Lorna had not spoken to a doctor. She had not spoken to anyone about how she was feeling. Instead, she had come to the lonely conclusion that it would be simpler for everybody if she climbed to the top of a parking garage . . . and threw herself off.

● ● ●

So this was why she was here, Jessica thought. This was what had been drawing her back to the hospital each night. Suddenly it all made sense. She was here to stop Lorna from jumping. To stop her making the mistake she had made herself, but . . . there was a problem.

Lorna could not hear her. Jessica called across the parking garage, then shouted and waved and finally moved over to the figure sitting on the parapet and floated in the air in front of her, urging her to move back to safety, begging her to think again. But Lorna could neither hear nor see her. Why this should be so— why the one person who most *needed* to hear her could not—Jessica did not know. But Lorna clearly had not the least idea that she was there.

Jessica thought of her friends. If she could tell Francis, Andi, or Roland what was happening, they would be able to call for help. Or they could come up here and talk to Lorna themselves. Tell her that they knew, better than most people, how she felt.

But her friends were still in a car somewhere on the road, traveling back from the theater. She quickly thought herself to Roland's house, to see if they had returned early, then checked at Alma Road in case Mrs. Boyle had gone there first, but there was no sign of them, and Jessica returned to the parking garage. She sat beside Lorna on the parapet and wondered desperately what else she could do.

Who else might be able to help?

And suddenly, without thinking, she found herself back in her old bedroom in Aunt Jo's house. One moment she was sitting with Lorna in the parking garage, and the next she was standing in the corner of the room where her bed used to be, while opposite her, Aunt Jo was sitting at the desk by the window, writing a letter on the computer.

"Auntie?" said Jessica. "Auntie, can you help?"

Aunt Jo did not answer, and the only sound was of her fingers tapping at the keys.

"Auntie!" Jessica found herself shouting. "It's an emergency, please! You have to help!"

But shouting made no more difference here than it had in the parking garage with Lorna. Aunt Jo could not hear her, and Jessica felt a rising frustration. "You've *got* to hear me!" she yelled at the top of her voice. "I need you to help! She's going to kill herself!" She stepped forward and tried to grab her aunt's shoulders, but of course there was nothing to grab. Her hands slid straight through her body . . .

. . . and Aunt Jo stopped typing.

With her hands frozen above the keys, she lifted her head to one side, as if she thought she had heard something.

Jessica moved her body very close to her aunt's, so that the two of them almost merged.

"Listen," she spoke directly into her aunt's ear. "You have to go to the hospital. Do you hear me? Lorna's going to kill herself and you have to go there. You have to go there *now*!"

Aunt Jo still did not move.

"Oh, come on!" In a gesture of frustration, Jessica swept her hand through the computer and, with a brief *plink*, it turned itself off. "Listen to me! You have to go to the hospital. The hospital! You have to go there. There's no one else. You have to stop her . . ."

There was a bemused look on Aunt Jo's face as she turned in her chair and looked carefully around the room.

"The hospital . . . You have to go to the hospital . . . You have to go there now . . ." Jessica was repeating the same phrases over and over again, half of her body still merged with her aunt's.

And Aunt Jo, still with that slightly puzzled look on her face, stood up. Jessica followed her as she left the room and walked slowly downstairs. She stopped in the hallway to put her head around the sitting room door.

"I'm just going out, George," she said, and without waiting for a reply, picked up a set of car keys and walked out of the front door.

● ● ●

Lorna was exactly as Jessica had left her, sitting on the parapet with her bag and her stuffed dog, staring out over the town.

Jessica sat down beside her.

"It's going to be okay," she said. "Aunt Jo's on her way. She'll know what to do. She's done training in this sort of thing. You just have to wait till she gets here. Fifteen minutes, that's all."

She hoped that she was right. She had followed her aunt down to the front door and watched her climb into the little car parked in the driveway. She had sat in the passenger seat while Aunt Jo had set off on the road to the hospital, but then decided to return to Lorna.

Not that there was much she could do now that she was here. Lorna still gave no sign of being able to hear what she was saying, but Jessica kept talking anyway. She told Lorna about her own experiences, about her mother and her grandmother and about coming to live with Aunt Jo and Uncle George. She told her about dying and being a ghost and being stuck and, as the minutes ticked away, she began to think it might be all right.

Then, with the hands on the big clock on the hospital tower behind them showing five to eleven, Lorna took a deep breath and stood up. She stood on the parapet, the warm breeze riffling her hair and clothes, stared down at the concrete below, and took a half step forward.

"No!" Jessica cried out. Aunt Jo would not be here for another five minutes at least. "No, you mustn't! You mustn't! You have to wait!" She floated up to stand in front of Lorna, pushing her back with hands that disappeared into Lorna's chest. "You're not going to make the same mistake I made. I won't let you . . ."

Lorna could not hear her, but as Jessica continued to shout and plead, she could see in the girl's eyes the same puzzled expression that had been on her aunt's face. As if some tiny part of her was aware of what was being said, though her conscious mind had no idea what it was.

27

When Mrs. Boyle got back from Southampton, a little before eleven, she dropped Francis and Andi off on Alma Road. Francis was climbing out of the back- seat, still saying thank you, when Jessica appeared behind him.

"Francis! You have to help!"

"Jessica?" He spun around. "What is it? What's the matter?"

"It's Lorna. Lorna Gilchrist. She's the other one."

"The other what?" Andi was climbing out of the car to join him. "What's happening?"

"Lorna's on the top floor of the parking garage at the hospital. She's going to jump." Jessica already had the feeling it was taking too long to explain all this. "You have to come up there. Now. She can't hear me!"

"You want us to . . ."

"The hospital parking garage. Top floor. Now!" shouted Jessica, and she was gone.

"Is everything all right?" Mrs. Boyle had wound down her window and was looking anxiously up at Francis.

"Yes," he said. "I'm sorry, but I wonder . . . could you drive us to the hospital?"

"The hospital? Why? Are you feeling ill?"

"It's not me," said Francis, "but something bad is going to happen at the parking garage, and it's very important we get there as quickly as possible. Can you drive us?"

If it had been anyone else, Mrs. Boyle would have wanted the answers to a great many questions before she drove anywhere, but this was Francis making the request, and all she did was turn on the ignition and put the car into gear.

"Don't forget your seat belts," she said, as she pulled out into the road.

It took a little under two minutes to drive the mile and a half to the hospital. As they drove up the hill, Roland, peering out of the windshield from the passenger seat, was the first to see the small figure silhouetted against the dark sky at the top of the parking garage.

"There she is," he pointed. "Up there."

Mrs. Boyle swung the car up a ramp to the entrance and halted in front of the barrier. She was about to suggest that it might be quicker for Francis to walk from there, but he and Andi were already out of the car and running through the entrance.

A pair of arms shot out and grabbed each of them by the collar. The security man had emerged from his post and his beefy hands were firmly clasped around the tops of their shirts.

"And where," he said, "do you two think you're . . ."

He never finished the sentence. Nor did he see the blows that landed somewhere below his belt. All he knew was that he could no longer breathe or walk. His grip on the two children loosened and he toppled to the ground.

"I'll deal with him," said Andi, already kneeling beside the body. "You go and look after Lorna."

Francis went racing toward the stairs. Roland came over from the car and, under Andi's instructions, helped lift the security man into a sitting position, with his back resting against a concrete post.

"What . . . what happened?" he gasped, when he was finally able to breathe.

"It looked to me like you tripped over the curb there," said Mrs. Boyle, standing over him. "But I'm sure you'll be all right when you've had a bit of a rest." She took her phone from her pocket and looked at Andi. "I hope no one minds, but I'm going to call the police."

• • •

Francis emerged from the staircase onto the top floor of the parking garage and saw Lorna standing on the parapet away to his right. She was poised with her toes over the edge and lifting her arms like a diver getting ready to jump. Directly in front of her, their bodies almost blended together, floated Jessica's ghost.

"Lorna?" he called. "Lorna, what are you doing?"

Lorna gave no sign that she had heard him, but she stopped moving.

"Please," said Francis. "Please . . . Come down from there."

There was still no response, though Lorna did at least remain still.

"You want me to run and grab her?" A breathless Andi had appeared behind Francis.

"You'd better not come too close," Jessica called. "Just stay where you are, and keep talking."

It was all very well to say keep talking, Francis thought, but what about? What on earth was he supposed to say?

"You don't have to do this." He began moving slowly toward the parapet as he spoke, but still keeping his distance from Lorna. "Really, you don't. Whatever's wrong, I'm sure we can do something about it, if you'll just come down from there. There's people we can go to. People we can tell . . ."

The words petered out. He remembered how he had felt in the weeks before Jessica had appeared. How unhappy he had been and how certain that nobody could do anything to help at all.

"Look, I know how you feel," he said. "Really I do. And I'm sorry. I wish I'd known before. I wish any of us had known. If we'd known we could have . . . we could have . . . Look, please . . . please come down . . . please . . ."

It was no good. He simply had no idea what to say to the girl in front of him. Maybe Andi was right. Maybe their best chance was to run as fast as they could and try and grab her before she jumped.

He took a step forward and a hand descended on his shoulder. He looked around to see a tall woman with short black hair standing just behind him.

"Not too close," said Aunt Jo softly. "Not yet." She called across to Lorna. "Hello, Lorna? My name is Joanna Barfield. I've come to ask if there's anything I can do to help. I know it probably seems like there's nothing anybody can do, but it might be worth hanging on for a moment just to listen. In case there *is* something. Believe it or not, I've spoken to quite a few people who feel like you do and . . . would you like to hear what I said to them?"

Lorna did not answer, but Aunt Jo did not seem to mind. She simply carried on talking. Afterward, neither Francis nor Andi could remember much of what she actually said, but Francis always claimed she had one of the calmest, quietest voices he had ever heard. The words flowed out of her mouth like gently running water.

Occasionally, she would ask a question and at first there were no replies, but then she said something about having a niece who had felt the same way and Lorna turned, briefly, to face her. After that, some questions got an occasional nod or shake of the head, and still Aunt Jo went on talking and asking questions, but now Lorna started replying to some of them. At first, it was only a yes or a no, but then it was an occasional sentence and still Aunt Jo's voice went on, gentle as falling snow, persistent as the rain.

Part of Francis was aware that, behind him, others had made their way onto the roof of the parking garage. He had heard sirens—the result of Roland's mother calling the police—and there was the rustle of clothes and the sound of whispering, but neither he nor Andi had dared to turn around. Their eyes were glued to Lorna's feet, poised on the edge of the parapet.

And Aunt Jo was still talking. Her soft, reassuring tones never paused for a moment, and now she was moving closer and it was Lorna doing most of the speaking. In a voice full of rage and anger and despair, she was talking about the stories that Angela and Denise had told, those wicked, wicked stories, those terrible lies—and Aunt Jo was leading Francis across to where she stood and then Francis was helping her down from the parapet and Aunt Jo was holding the sobbing girl in her arms and telling her it was all right. It was all right. It was all going to be all right . . .

A policewoman appeared with a blanket, which she wrapped around Lorna's shoulders, and she and Aunt Jo led Lorna back across the parking garage, to where a woman Francis recognized as Lorna's mother was waiting.

28

There was a quarter of an hour or so after that when no one seemed to take much notice of either Francis or Andi. The top floor of the parking garage was full of an extraordinary number of people. There were policemen, paramedics, nurses, and at least half a dozen security men, including the one from downstairs, walking with a slight limp. Two of the paramedics were putting Lorna onto a gurney—a process complicated by the fact that she refused to let go of Aunt Jo—while her mother was shouting angrily at any policeman who would listen that "something ought to be done."

Francis and Andi walked over to where Jessica was sitting on the parapet.

"You got here just in time," said Jessica. "Another few seconds and she'd have done it."

"It was your aunt who stopped her." Francis picked up the stuffed dog and gently rearranged its paws. "She was amazing. If she hadn't turned up, I think . . ." He paused. "Which reminds me, how *did* she turn up? Who told her to come here?"

"I think I did," said Jessica.

"I thought she couldn't see you?"

"She couldn't." Jessica gave a shrug. "Don't ask me to explain. I don't understand it either."

"I told you!" Roland was striding over to join them. "I said there'd be another one." He grinned at Jessica. "That's why you were here, so you could . . ." He stopped. "Are you all right?"

"I am now," said Jessica. "Why?"

"You . . . um . . . you . . ." Roland was not sure how to say it, but Jessica did look rather strange. Her skin had acquired an odd, slightly luminous glow. You could see it in her hands and her face. It was a white light with a faint tinge of gold and, as he stared, the light became stronger.

"You look as if you're on fire," said Andi.

They watched in silence as the light from Jessica's body grew brighter and brighter. Soon, it was strong enough to actually shine through her clothes.

"Jessica?" Francis sounded thoroughly alarmed. "What's happening?"

But Jessica did not answer. She was staring across at the hospital, at one of the windows on the third floor, and Francis had to repeat his question twice before she slowly turned to face him.

"I'm sorry," she said. "I think I have to go now."

"Go? Go where?" The light from Jessica's body was now bright enough to make his eyes water, and it was a moment before he understood what she meant. "Oh . . . oh, you mean . . . *go*!"

Jessica nodded.

"Do you have to?" said Francis. "I mean, can't you stay a little longer?"

"No. No, I can't." By now Jessica's body was a beacon that, for them, lit up every corner of the parking garage. "But don't worry. It's all right."

She took a step toward Francis, reached out, and put her arms around him. To his astonishment, she felt quite solid. In a funny way, Francis said afterward, she felt more solid than he did himself. As if she were the one with the real body, and he were merely the ghost.

"If you only knew," she whispered in his ear. "If any of us had only known . . ."

She held him for a moment, then let him go. She smiled at the others and began floating through the air toward the hospital. Outside the little window of the room on the third floor, they saw her turn for one last time, give a little wave . . . and she was gone.

• • •

Francis, Andi, and Roland were still standing there when Aunt Jo came over to join them. She looked at Francis. "I've just remembered where I've seen you before," she said. "You're the boy who was standing outside my house, aren't you?"

"Yes," said Francis.

"Can I ask how you came to be here tonight?"

Francis didn't know what to say.

"I only ask," said Aunt Jo, "because the lady over there"—she pointed to Roland's mother, talking to a policeman—"tells me you suddenly announced that you knew something bad was going to happen at the hospital. And much the same thing happened to me."

"Did it?"

"Yes. I was sitting at my desk at home, and I had this feeling that I should get in the car and drive here.

It was almost like someone was telling me to come. Is that what happened to you?"

"Pretty much," said Francis.

"It's a strange world." Aunt Jo shook her head. "I don't even pretend to understand it." They stood there for a moment, staring out over the town. "I don't know if you know, but my niece committed suicide."

"Yes," said Francis, "I had heard."

"I wish she'd had a friend like you turn up when she . . ." Aunt Jo paused for a moment. "Her name was Jessica. She was a lovely girl. I think, if you'd known her, you two would have gotten along rather well."

"Yes," said Francis, "I know we would."

29

At school the following Monday, Francis found he had become something of a celebrity. The story had made the six o'clock news on Sunday evening, and on Monday morning the *Daily Mail* ran it on its front page, along with a picture showing Lorna silhouetted against the night sky, while Francis reached out a hand to help her down.

The pictures had been taken by a hospital porter on his cell phone and, because he had been standing on the concrete pavement at the base of the parking garage when he took the video, Francis and Lorna were the only people in the picture. Neither Andi nor Jessica's aunt Jo were visible, and it somehow gave the impression that Francis had conducted the rescue entirely on his own. He kept telling people this wasn't true, but nobody seemed to take any notice.

When he arrived at school that morning, his home-room teacher shook his hand when he came into the classroom and told him how proud she was before sending him off to see Mrs. Parsons. On his way there, several other people stopped him in the corridor to congratulate him, and when he got to the office, the women who worked there stood up and gave him a round of applause. Karen, the receptionist, even insisted on giving him a hug before showing him in to see the principal.

Mrs. Parsons was a little more restrained, but she smiled as she asked him to sit down and offered him a cup of tea.

"It looks like you had a rather eventful weekend," she said, gesturing to a copy of the *Daily Mail* on her desk. "I've read about what happened, of course, but I'd be very interested to hear your account, if you wouldn't mind going over it again."

Francis said he didn't mind at all, and he told Mrs. Parsons the same story he had given the reporter from the *Mail*. It was completely truthful, except that it said nothing about Jessica or the way she had warned him. He simply said he had been coming back from Southampton with Andi and Roland when they had seen Lorna on the roof of the hospital parking garage.

"You recognized her?" Mrs. Parsons asked. "Even from that distance. In the dark?"

Francis said quite truthfully that, yes, he had known at once who it was. He went on to describe how he had run up the stairs, seen Lorna about to dive off the edge of the parapet, and called out for her to stop. Again, he said nothing about finding Jessica there. It was something he had discussed with the others, and they had all agreed that it was best. He told Mrs. Parsons how he had started talking to Lorna, but then run out of things to say, and how a woman—a Mrs. Barfield— had appeared, and eventually persuaded Lorna back from the edge. "I know it looks different in the picture," he said, "but really she was the one who did everything."

When he had finished, Mrs. Parsons took off her glasses, twirled them for a moment between her finger and thumb, and stared thoughtfully out the window.

"I knew there was something," she said eventually. She sounded, Francis thought, rather tired. "I knew there was something going on in that class, but I always thought the people at risk were you and Andi. Not

Lorna." She gave a long sigh. "I never saw it. I never saw it at all."

• • •

The newspaper report had given all the details of why Lorna had wanted to kill herself, and described it as a case of attempted bullycide. Lorna had tried to end her life, they said, because two girls at her school had been inventing stories about her. They did not give the girls' names, but the days that followed were not an easy time for Angela and Denise.

They tried very hard to pretend they had done nothing wrong. They came into school that Monday with every appearance of being as worried and concerned about poor Lorna as everyone else. They could be heard wondering who the two girls in the paper could possibly be. Who, they asked, could have done such a dreadful thing?

The girls were good liars. They were interviewed at length by Mrs. Parsons on three separate occasions, but stuck determinedly to their story that they had only ever passed on gossip that had been told them by someone else. Nobody was really fooled but, for a while, it looked as if they might get away with it. Then on Wednesday, they didn't come in to school.

It turned out the girls had been swapping their ideas for stories about Lorna in a series of messages that the police had found on their computers. They were expelled from school the same day and Mrs. Parsons announced in assembly that the expulsion would be permanent. It would not be fair, she said, to ask Lorna to return to school while Angela and Denise were still there, so they would have to continue their education somewhere else.

Lorna was in the hospital for a week, at home for a month, and, in the end, did not come back to John Felton at all. Mrs. Parsons did her best to reassure her that things would be different if she did, but Lorna steadfastly refused. She went instead to a private school, where the principal, who had read about her case, had offered her a scholarship. It was, oddly enough, the same private school at which Andi had been so unhappy—but Lorna loved it from the first day she arrived. She was a popular and successful pupil there, eventually becoming head girl and winning a place to study natural sciences at Cambridge.

30

Francis did not find it easy, being a celebrity, but he got used to it. He found it much harder to get used to being without Jessica. Andi and Roland missed her as well, but it was hardest for Francis. For the last five months, she had been the most important person in his life and, now that she was gone, he missed her more than he could say.

Up in his attic room, there were reminders of her wherever he looked. She was there in most of the drawings on the walls. She was there in the half-finished shift dress by the sewing machine. She was almost there, sitting on the sofa, when he came up the stairs and walked into the room . . . except that she wasn't. She wasn't anywhere. Because she'd gone.

At times, the sadness of that thought threatened to overwhelm him, and a part of him was frightened that life might go back to how it had been before she first appeared . . . but it didn't. He felt sad, very sad, that his friend was no longer with him, but somehow it was never like being in The Pit. For reasons he did not understand, it was a different sort of sad.

There were two things that helped. The first was that Andi and Roland took no notice when he said that he didn't want to see anyone and that he wanted to be alone. Andi simply took him by the arm and told him there wasn't much chance of that.

"No chance at all," Roland agreed. "You're stuck with us now. Whether you like it or not."

And Francis found, as the days passed, that he did like it. As the pain lessened, he even began to realize that having friends who stuck was one of the best things that could happen to you.

The second thing that helped, though in a more roundabout way, was the letters. They had started arriving the day after the story featured on the news and, a month later, were still coming.

A lot of them just wanted to congratulate Francis on what he had done, but a good many asked for his advice. They were from parents worried that their children might be thinking of doing what Lorna had done, and wanting to know how to stop them. Or from teenagers who said they were going through the same things that had happened to Lorna, and asking Francis what they should do.

Francis had no idea how to answer them. Apart from anything else, there were so many. Within a week, there were over a hundred piled up on the table in his attic room, and he knew he could never reply to them all. Even if he could, what was he supposed to say? What *could* you say to someone who told you they were thinking of killing themselves? He hadn't known what to say to Lorna on the roof, so how could he be qualified to give advice now? He showed the letters to his mother, who said she had no idea how to answer them either, but pointed out that there was one person who might.

"That woman who appeared on the roof of the parking garage," she said. "Mrs. Barfield. Didn't she turn out to be a trained counselor or something?"

Aunt Jo came over that evening after school, and instantly offered to take the letters away and sort them.

"I'll start by grading them for you," she said, "so you'll know which are the most important and which you can leave for a bit. Then if you come over on the weekend, we can start working on replies to the ones that are really urgent."

That weekend, Francis went out to Aunt Jo's house, and the two of them sat in the room that had once been Jessica's bedroom and he tapped out replies on the computer, while Mrs. Barfield advised him on what to say. In most cases the advice she gave was fairly obvious— the need to talk to someone, and get proper help—but Aunt Jo said that, just because it was obvious, didn't mean it wasn't important.

They worked out an order of priority for the letters, and Francis found he enjoyed writing his answers. It was a good thing to be doing, the sort of thing Jessica would have approved of, he thought, if she was still around, and he went out to Aunt Jo's house most weekends, doing a few more letters each time. In fact, he even turned down the opportunity to go to Canada for a month, so that he could carry on doing it through summer vacation.

• • •

It was Andi's mother who had organized the trip to Canada. Sitting in the kitchen one evening with Francis and his mother, she announced in her booming voice that she had a brother who lived on a farm near Calgary.

"Andi loves it out there," she said. "So we're going out for four weeks in August."

Francis wondered if anyone else had noticed that Mrs. Campion no longer called her daughter Thug or Thuglette. She had been "Andi" for some time now.

"But she doesn't want to go without you." Mrs. Campion looked across at Francis. "So I wondered if you'd come with us. Roland's already agreed."

Francis hesitated.

"You don't have to worry about the money," said his mother. "We can afford it. You wouldn't believe what Frieda is charging for my plates these days!"

"And there'll be lots to do out there," said Mrs. Campion, persuasively. "It's a huge farm, and there'll be horse-riding, canoeing, white-water rafting, mountain climbing . . ."

Francis wondered how Roland would cope with canoeing and white-water rafting, and then thought he would probably cope rather well. As long as he was near Andi, Roland would have happily rafted over Niagara Falls.

"But neither of them wants to go without you," said Mrs. Campion, "so will you think about it, at least?"

Francis agreed that he would, but in the end announced that, though grateful for the offer, he would rather stay at home. He was not really a canoeing, white-water rafting sort of person, he explained, and he preferred to spend the summer working with Aunt Jo on answering his letters.

And this time, not even Andi and Roland could persuade him to change his mind.

31

On the Tuesday after school ended, Andi and Roland left for Canada. Francis went to wave them off from Gatwick Airport and wondered, when he got back, if he had made the right choice. Sitting in his room at the top of the house on Alma Road, he suddenly felt rather lonely.

He did not have the chance to feel lonely for long, however, because Roland's mother appeared the next morning to drive him out to Aunt Jo's. She had offered to do this each day, partly because she liked to have someone to talk to about Roland, but also because it meant Francis could help her sort out any problems she was having with her work for her exams.

Francis went out to Aunt Jo's every morning, Monday to Friday, and once he was there the two of them would sit in the office and set about answering the next batch of letters.

Some of them were from people who had undergone abuse, or been physically harmed, or had illnesses that left them in constant pain—and when Francis read them, it was easy to see why the writer had been driven to the point of despair. And a relief that Aunt Jo always seemed to find something encouraging to say, and to suggest a person or an organization that she thought might be able to help.

But what struck Francis most forcibly was how many of the letters came from people who were *not* being starved or beaten or living with chronic pain, but who were, nevertheless, desperately unhappy. They were from people like Roland, who thought they were too fat, or like Andi, who thought they weren't pretty. Or people like himself, who knew they were just . . . *different*. The reasons they gave for this feeling were as numerous as the letters themselves, but that was the one thing they all had in common. All the people who wrote described how they felt separated somehow from the world around them.

Alone.

And *different*.

Why, Francis wondered, should being different be so painful? Why did it matter so much when, if you thought about it, everybody was different in one way or another?

"I think," said Aunt Jo, when he asked her, "that some people feel these things more than most of us. They're more sensitive. But I also think the real damage comes when you add in something else. If someone's already feeling low for some reason and *then* they lose a parent like Jessica did, or get ill, or if you throw a Denise Ritchie and an Angela Wyman into the mix—that's when it can get serious." She passed over the letter she had been reading from a boy who was being bullied because he had taken up knitting.

"This one's your department, I think," she said.

Francis liked being in what had once been Jessica's room. He liked looking at the photos of her that hung on the wall. And he liked hearing Aunt Jo talking about her, telling him stories of things she had done while she was alive.

"I sometimes feel that she's still here," Aunt Jo told him one day. "You know . . . like she comes in occasionally to check up on what I'm doing. And I've always thought she was the one who told me to come out to the hospital that night. Do you think that's silly?"

And Francis said no, he didn't think it was silly at all.

• • •

Aunt Jo would only allow Francis to work on the letters in the mornings. She said it wasn't good for him to be doing that sort of thing all day and insisted that after lunch he go off and have some fun with people his own age. Francis wanted to point out that the only friends he had of his own age were on the other side of the Atlantic, but in a short space of time that wasn't exactly true.

Mrs. Parsons phoned him a week into the holidays. "I've got a problem," she said. "There's a youth drama group using the school over the summer—they're doing *West Side Story*—and they need some help. Are you busy at the moment?"

"I'm not much good at acting," said Francis.

"No, no, they don't want you for that!" Mrs. Parsons chuckled. "The last thing they need is another prima donna. But they are a bit stuck on costumes. And I seem to remember that's something you're quite good at."

Francis agreed to take a look at the problem, and that afternoon he walked to the school, where some twenty or thirty teenagers were gathered in the main hall tapping out a dance number that involved a lot of swirling skirts and stamping feet. The woman in charge was called Mrs. Wigley, and she told Francis that the person who normally did their costumes was in the hospital having a baby.

"We were hoping she'd hold off until all this was over," said Mrs. Wigley, "but she was caught short yesterday, right in the middle of a rather complicated fight scene." She led the way out of the hall and into a classroom that was filled with costumes hanging on racks. "We've rented most of the stuff, but of course none of it fits. What we need is some whiz with a needle and thread who can sort it all out." She looked hopefully at Francis. "Any chance you could help?"

Ten minutes later, Francis was sitting at a table with a sewing machine, and for the next three weeks found himself altering, cutting, nipping, and tucking, and sometimes tearing whole costumes apart to make new ones. The experience was something of a revelation.

All the time he was there, not one of the people who came to have their costume fitted, not a single one, ever suggested that it was odd to have Francis doing the work. The only thing that any of them ever worried about was how they were going to look on stage, and once they found Francis was the person who could sort this out for them, he was treated with considerable respect. They would knock on the door to his room and ask apologetically if he could take in the waist on their pants, or find them a different-colored top. And when he did as they asked, they would tell him in extravagant language how wonderful he was and how grateful they were.

Sometimes, when they weren't needed on stage, they came into his room simply to talk. They would sit on one of the tables while he was darning a hole or mending a tear and tell him things about themselves that Francis would never have dared to tell his own mother. They behaved quite differently from anyone he had known before, and the biggest difference was that they seemed to *like* being different. It was not something that made them ashamed or unhappy. It was something they enjoyed.

The show ran for a week and was a huge success. After it was over, Mrs. Wigley told Francis that she thought the success was almost entirely due to his wonderful costumes and, even though he heard her tell the man who played the piano that it was mostly due to his music, he didn't mind. He had loved every moment of it and, as everyone hugged and kissed each other good-bye on the last night, he readily agreed that he would be around next year to do it all again.

Jessica, he couldn't help thinking, would have loved it.

● ● ●

Two days later, Andi and Roland came back from Canada. Both of them were barely recognizable. It took Francis several seconds to realize that the figure hurtling toward him across the arrivals lounge was Andi. She had dyed her hair blond, her skin was deeply tanned, and she was wearing a short flouncy skirt with a halter-neck top in colors that were deliberately chosen, she told him later, so that he would have something to criticize. She leaped on him from a distance of several feet and held him in a grip that drove every ounce of breath from his body.

Roland looked even stranger. He was several inches taller, twenty pounds lighter, and exuded the sort of confidence that only comes from hiking through mountains, rappelling down cliffs, and canoeing through white-water gorges. He was bigger than ever, but in a different way. Detaching himself from his mother, he came over to say hello.

"Hi, man . . ." His voice was big and deep as he grinned down at Francis. "How's it been?"

As they drove back to the house, swapping stories of play productions and encounters with grizzly bears, it was clear that one thing at least had not changed. The three were as close friends as ever. Everything else in his life might have altered, Francis thought, but it was good to know that some things had stayed the same.

32

Quite how much everything else had changed Francis did not fully realize until the start of the autumn term a few days later. It was a lunchtime, and he was sitting on the bench by the playing field, enjoying the heat of the sun and sewing up the hem of a skirt for a girl in ninth grade.

The girl was Rowena Evans and she had been in the drama group in the summer, singing and dancing as one of the Jets. The skirt was something her grandmother had bought her that didn't fit properly, so she had asked Francis if he would mind making a few alterations.

Francis had been happy to oblige, and he was already halfway around the hem when a shadow fell across his work. Looking up, he saw a boy about his own age standing in front of him.

"What are you doing?" asked the boy.

"I'm sewing," said Francis.

The boy stared down at him. "Only girls sew," he said.

"Interestingly enough," said Francis, "the idea that sewing is girls' work is comparatively recent. My great-great-grandfather was in the navy, and in his day, the men never left that sort of thing to a woman. They thought they weren't neat enough."

The boy gave a snort of derision. His name was Kevin and he and his family had recently moved down from Sheffield. At his old school, if a boy had been seen sewing a girl's skirt, they would never have gotten home alive.

"You wouldn't catch me doing it," he said.

"No," Francis agreed. "Probably not."

Kevin continued to stare at him for a moment; then, shaking his head in disbelief, he wandered away.

"What did he want?" Roland had sat himself down on the bench beside Francis.

"Nothing really," said Francis. "He thought it was a bit odd to see me sewing."

"He wasn't bothering you, was he?" Andi sat herself the other side of him and pulled open the lid of her lunch box. "Because if he was, Rollie and I would be very happy to have a word with him."

"It's okay," said Francis. "He wasn't any bother."

And it was true. The encounter with Kevin hadn't bothered him in the least, which was odd if you thought how much it would have mattered at the start of the year. He wondered what it was, exactly, that had changed.

Roland was unpacking his lunch.

"It's sliced avocado and Brie in whole-wheat baguettes," he said when Andi asked, "with green peppers, sliced tomatoes, and a drizzle of olive oil." The lunches Mrs. Boyle made for her son were rather different these days, but they were still mouthwateringly delicious.

Quite a few things had changed in the last eight months, thought Francis, and it wasn't easy to say which had made the most difference. It certainly helped to have friends—particularly friends as dauntingly large as Roland or as scary as Andi—but it wasn't just that . . .

The school itself felt different these days. Ever since Lorna had tried to jump off the top of the hospital parking garage, the staff took any form of bullying very seriously, and these days, Francis knew if he was ever bothered by jokes from someone like Quentin and reported the fact, it would be taken very seriously. Mrs. Parsons had made it abundantly clear that the right to feel safe at school was one of her top priorities, and there were several initiatives to help make sure that it happened.

But it wasn't just that either . . .

"Let's swap," Andi told Roland. "You can have some of my lunch and I'll have some of yours."

"What's in it?" Roland asked, peering inside the sandwich Andi had given him.

"Jam," said Andi. "Red jam. Come on, hand it over . . ."

The biggest change, Francis thought, wasn't in either his friends or in the school, but in himself. The real reason that it didn't bother him when someone laughed at him for sewing a skirt wasn't that he knew he could tell Mrs. Parsons, or that Andi would come to his rescue. It was because it didn't *matter* what other people thought anymore. If they said that what he was doing was funny and wanted to laugh . . . then let them. After all, it *was* a bit funny. And different. But that was how he was, and the people around him would have to live with it.

And the strange thing was that, now that he didn't really care what other people thought, most of them seemed quite happy to let him be as different as he liked. They might see what he was doing, as Kevin had done, and make the odd remark, but because he didn't mind they tended, as Kevin had done, to drift away. If anyone made a habit of making remarks like that, he might have to do something about it, but it hadn't happened yet, and Francis had a feeling it probably never would.

"I suppose you want some as well?" Beside him, Roland was holding out a twelve-inch chunk of bread with soft cheese dripping from the edges.

"Oh, thanks . . ." Francis took it absentmindedly. They always wound up eating Roland's lunch. Mrs. Boyle made healthier food for him these days, but had never quite conquered the habit of making three times more than was needed.

So many changes and they had all, when you looked back on it, happened so fast. It was something he often talked about in the letters he still wrote at Aunt Jo's house to the people who emailed her website—the speed with which life could change. How it could appear so impossible at one moment, and so full of hope and possibilities the next.

And you never knew how or when that change might happen, thought Francis. You never knew what was around the corner in life and what it might throw up next. You never knew when someone like Jessica was about to walk over and sit herself down on the bench beside you . . .

That was how the change had happened in his own life, of course. It had all started on the day Jessica joined him on the bench. Meeting Andi and Roland, sorting out Quentin, saving Lorna—it had all begun with Jessica. She was the one who had set the change in motion. She was the one who had taught him how much fun there was to be had in life, how full of opportunities it was, how many chances it gave for enjoyment . . .

It was an odd lesson to have learned from someone who was dead.

And it was a shame she wasn't here to see the results of the changes she had caused. Francis often thought how much she would have enjoyed seeing Roland these days as he strode, big and confident, through the school. How she would have loved to see Andi, with a huge smile covering her face, firmly telling them both what they would be doing that weekend . . .

Though if you believed Aunt Jo, of course, maybe she *could* see them. Maybe she checked in on them once in a while, to see how they were doing. Maybe she had been watching through that little exchange with Kevin. Maybe . . . maybe she was there right now.

The sun shone warm on his back and he could feel the heat of it spreading through his jacket into his shoulders. It was a gentle, relaxing warmth, and he sat back on the bench and took a big bite of the sandwich Roland had given him.

It was, like so many things in life these days, absolutely delicious.

Acknowledgments

One of the great dividing lines among writers is between those who simply sit down and start writing—with no firm idea of where their story is going—and those who like to plan the whole thing out beforehand. They know what will be in each chapter (sometimes in each paragraph) and before they have penned the first sentence, they know *exactly* how the story will end.

I am definitely in the planning camp, though I have a sneaking admiration for those who dare to launch into a story, writing thousands of words, in the simple trust that their artistic intuition will eventually ensure that all the threads come together in a satisfying resolution. It's a technique, I know, that produces the best as well as the worst of writing, but I only tried it once myself—and this book was the result. I started with the idea of a girl who was dead (without knowing why) meeting a boy . . . and just took it from there.

I was halfway through the book before I discovered how Jessica had died and then, suddenly, the fact that she had befriended Francis, Andi, and Roland made alarming sense. I say "alarming" because this was not my sort of story at all. I write comedy, really—light comedy—and this whole topic was way, way too serious for someone like me. It wasn't as if I knew anything about suicide in the first place . . .

It took ten years for the story to achieve the form you can read in this book. It helped, more than anyone not in the business can know, to have an agent like Hilary Delamere to nudge it into an acceptable form— to have an editor like Bella Pearson gently pointing out the bits that could do with a bit of a rethink, and to have the legendary David Fickling firing you up with his extraordinary enthusiasm. There is something about working with such very classy people that makes you up your game. I still have the umpteen earlier drafts on my computer as painful evidence of how much their help was needed.

As I said, I have never contemplated suicide myself, but I do know a bit about depression and, for some years, had regular visits from what Churchill called the Black Dog. At such times, I was immensely grateful for the presence of those who were prepared, patiently, to stand beside me until the clouds dispersed and the sunshine returned. And even more grateful to those, like Jessica in this book, whose mere presence was a constant reminder that, even at its darkest, life is full of possibilities and that, yes, miracles can happen.

And do.

Andrew Norriss
Chilbolton, England
2014